The Giant Rat of Sumatra

Al, the stagehand, appeared in the doorway and said, "We're getting ready to run through the transformation scene. Places, please."

Standing in the wings, Joe began to feel excited. He had watched this scene half a dozen times, but he was still captivated by the magic that transformed a London street into the shadowy interior of a sinister warehouse.

As the lighting changed in color and intensity, the turntable started to revolve. The set that represented the warehouse came into view. As it did, Joe saw a limp figure lying half on, half off the turntable, legs dragging along the floorboards.

Then Joe's eyes widened. As the figure drew closer, it began to look terribly familiar. Even in the dim light, Joe couldn't mistake the face of his brother.

With mounting horror, he saw that Frank was being dragged toward a wooden column, one of the platform supports. In another moment, his legs would be caught between the wall of the revolving set and the column.

He'd be crushed!

The Hardy Boys Mystery Stories

Available from MINSTREL Books

THE HARDY BOYS®

143

THE GIANT RAT OF SUMATRA

FRANKLIN W. DIXON

A MINSTREL® BOOK

Published by POCKET BOOKS

New York London Toronto Sydney Tokyo Singapore

The sale of this book without its cover is unauthorized. If you purchased
this book without a cover, you should be aware that it was reported to
the publisher as "unsold and destroyed." Neither the author nor the
publisher has received payment for the sale of this "stripped book."

This book is a work of fiction. Names, characters, places and
incidents are products of the author's imagination or are used
fictitiously. Any resemblance to actual events or locales or per-
sons, living or dead, is entirely coincidental.

A MINSTREL PAPERBACK *Original*

A Minstrel Book published by
POCKET BOOKS, a division of Simon & Schuster Inc.
1230 Avenue of the Americas, New York, NY 10020

Copyright © 1997 by Simon & Schuster Inc.

Front cover illustration by Lee McLeod

Produced by Mega-Books, Inc.

All rights reserved, including the right to reproduce
this book or portions thereof in any form whatsoever.
For information address Pocket Books, 1230 Avenue
of the Americas, New York, NY 10020

ISBN: 0-671-00055-1

First Minstrel Books printing April 1997

10 9 8 7 6 5 4 3 2 1

THE HARDY BOYS MYSTERY STORIES is a trademark
of Simon & Schuster Inc.

THE HARDY BOYS, A MINSTREL BOOK and colophon
are registered trademarks of Simon & Schuster Inc.

Printed in the U.S.A.

Contents

For orders other than by individual consumers, Pocket Books grants a discount on the purchase of **10 or more** copies of single titles for special markets or premium use. For further details, please write to the Vice-President of Special Markets, Pocket Books, 1633 Broadway, New York, NY 10019-6785, 8th Floor.

For information on how individual consumers can place orders, please write to Mail Order Department, Simon & Schuster Inc., 200 Old Tappan Road, Old Tappan, NJ 07675.

1 Joe Plays a Part

"Ready for a game of hoops?" Frank Hardy asked his younger brother, Joe, who was galloping down the stairs.

"I'm always ready," Joe said as he sat on the last step and tightened the laces of his hightops. "The question is, are you ready for me?"

"Face it," Frank said to Joe, who at seventeen was a year younger, "everything you know, you learned from me."

As the boys started down the hall, Frank saw that the door to their father's study was ajar.

"Dad?" Frank said, putting his head in the doorway. "We'll be— Oh, sorry. I didn't know you had a visitor."

"Come on in, Frank," Fenton Hardy said, get-

1

ting up from his desk. "You, too, Joe. I'd like you to meet Donald O'Lunny."

O'Lunny was a man of medium height with a short-cropped gray beard and a deep tan. He was wearing neatly creased jeans and a maroon turtleneck. He stood up and put out his hand.

Frank's eyes widened. "O'Lunny? Didn't you write that new musical about Sherlock Holmes?" he asked as they shook hands. *"The Giant Rat of Sumatra."*

O'Lunny smiled. "That's right. Are you and your brother theater fans?"

Joe brushed back his blond hair. "Well, not really," he admitted. "But we're crazy about anything that involves mysteries and detectives. And the title is *so* cool."

"Besides," Frank added, "Dad invited us to come with him to the performance tonight."

"I was just telling Donald about some of the cases you two have cracked," Fenton said.

Fenton Hardy, a famous private detective, had enlisted the help of his two sons on many tough cases. It had been natural for Frank and Joe to start investigating crimes and solving mysteries on their own. Though they were still teenagers, the brothers had become quite skilled at detective work.

"I'm impressed with your father's account of

2

your exploits," O'Lunny told them. He smiled. "Maybe I'll base my next musical on your careers—if there is a next one."

"What do you mean?" Frank asked.

"Donald seems to have a problem," Fenton said. "He came to ask me if I could help. Unfortunately, the case I'm on now is taking me to Seattle first thing in the morning. I suggested that you two might be able to give him a hand."

"What's the matter?" Frank asked. He and Joe settled on the couch and gave the man their full attention.

"I wish I could tell you," O'Lunny said. "It's more a mood than anything. I've come to expect things to go wrong with a new production. But this is something else entirely. I hate to say it, but I believe that somebody is deliberately trying to wreck my play."

"Who would want to do that?" Frank asked.

"I wish I knew," O'Lunny replied, sighing in exasperation. "Like most people, I've made a few enemies over the years. But I can't think of anybody who has it in for me to this extent. It's driving me crazy."

O'Lunny looked from Frank to Joe. "I'd like to have somebody from the outside, somebody with the eye of a detective, take a good look around. What do you say?"

Frank glanced over at Joe.

"Why not?" Joe said.

"Okay," Frank said. "But we'll need to spend a lot of time around the theater, and we'll need a good excuse for doing it."

O'Lunny nodded. "I was just thinking about that. I'm acting as co-producer as well as author. What I suggest is that I introduce one of you as my new personal assistant. As for the other . . . well, do you have any objection to performing onstage? Does either one of you have an interest in theater?"

Joe sat up in his seat. "Acting, you mean? Yeah! That's for me."

"Do you know about the Baker Street Irregulars?" O'Lunny continued. "They're a bunch of street kids who help Sherlock Holmes in his cases. I think I can convince my director that we need one more of them in the play than we thought."

The look of eagerness on Joe's face made Frank choke back a laugh. "I think Joe's just right for the part," Frank said, grinning. "As for me, I'd rather work offstage."

O'Lunny put out his hand again. "Welcome to the cast, Joe," he said. After glancing at his watch, he added, "I'd better get you over to the theater. You'll have a lot to do before tonight's curtain goes up."

4

"I'm ready," Joe said quickly. He took a step toward the door.

"Should I come, too?" Frank asked.

O'Lunny stroked his beard. "Maybe not," he said slowly. "If I bring both of you in at the same time, people might get suspicious. I'll spread the word that I have a new assistant starting tomorrow. Okay?"

"Sure. I'll count on Joe to fill me in on whatever he finds out," Frank said. He grinned at his brother and said, "You know what they say in show business, Joe. . . . Break a leg!"

As Joe rode down Bayport's Main Street with O'Lunny, he found himself looking at the old Orpheum Theater in a new way. Soon he'd be acting on its stage.

O'Lunny parked his little sports coupe in back of the theater, and he and Joe got out. Joe followed O'Lunny up a short flight of metal stairs and through the stage entrance.

After the bright sunlight, the gloomy backstage area seemed pitch-black. Joe stopped short. Up ahead, about thirty feet away, light spilled from the stage itself. As his eyes adjusted to the darkness, Joe followed the silhouette of O'Lunny toward the lit area. They stopped just offstage, in the wings.

A woman and two men were onstage, singing a

5

bouncy song in harmony. As his foot started tapping, Joe strained to follow the words:

"Kippers and eggs, kippers and eggs,
 Give hope to your heart and spring to
    your legs.
 Come morning, each Englishman wakes
    up and begs
 For a jolly big breakfast of kippers and
    eggs!"

"How do you like it?" O'Lunny whispered.

"Terrific," Joe replied. He looked past him at the singers. One of the men was tall and thin, with a glittering eye and a hook nose. The other was short and stout, with a round face and a bushy mustache. Joe had no trouble guessing that the tall man was playing Sherlock Holmes and the short one was Dr. Watson. The woman had gray hair, pulled back in a bun. Joe figured she was playing Mrs. Hudson, the housekeeper.

When the song ended, the three actors walked over to the far side of the stage and started talking to the rehearsal pianist. A woman with long black hair and Asian features joined them.

"That's Charles Battenberg playing Holmes," O'Lunny said. "And Ewan Gordean as Watson. Celia Hatteras is Mrs. Hudson. Fine actors, all of them. We were lucky to have them here."

Joe mentally repeated the names to himself: Battenberg, Gordean, Hatteras. He wanted to take notes, but he wasn't sure it would fit with his cover. "Who is the woman they're talking to?" he asked.

"Li Wei, our composer," O'Lunny told him. "I'll introduce you when she's done going over her notes with the actors. Oh, good. There's Gilbert Hornby, our producer and director. Gilbert—over here!" he called.

The man who came toward them was over six feet tall but walked with his head bent forward. His wavy gray hair didn't seem to fit with the thick black eyebrows that almost met in the middle.

After introductions were made, O'Lunny told Gilbert Hornby that Joe would be one of the Irregulars.

Hornby raised his eyebrows. "A new cast member on the day the play opens?" he said. "That's pretty irregular."

O'Lunny laughed at the pun and said, "I think the group looks too small now. Joe will fill it out nicely."

"Fine, fine," Hornby said, glancing around. "I'll get someone to show him the ropes. Susanna?"

A blond girl of about sixteen joined them. Hornby introduced the actor to Joe. She listened

7

to Hornby's explanation, then smiled and said, "Hi, Joe. Welcome to the funny farm. I hope you're as crazed as the rest of us. You'll never survive otherwise."

Hornby took O'Lunny by the elbow and led him away, talking in an undertone.

"Opening night jitters, I guess," Susanna said, watching the men walk off. "We've all got them. Come on—I'll take you to meet the gang."

"What part do you play?" Joe asked, as they walked down a dark narrow hallway.

"I'm Alice, the Rat's daughter," Susanna said.

Joe looked perplexed. "Isn't the giant rat an enormous jungle rodent in Southeast Asia?" he asked.

Susanna laughed. "Nobody knows what the Giant Rat is. Sir Arthur Conan Doyle had Watson mention it in the story 'The Sussex Vampire.' But Conan Doyle never wrote a book about the Giant Rat. He was teasing his readers, so anyone can have fun imagining what the Giant Rat was. I guess you haven't read O'Lunny's script yet."

Joe shook his head, and Susanna took a deep breath before explaining the plot. "Okay, the Giant Rat—that's my dad—used to live in Sumatra. He's now the boss of a gang of criminals in London's East End, during Queen Victoria's day. He has a grand plan for a crime spree, but he's afraid that it will be foiled by Sherlock Holmes.

8

So he sets a trap for Holmes. But Alice—that's me—has a crush on Charles, the leader of the Baker Street Irregulars. So when she finds out what her father has planned, she sends a secret warning to Holmes."

Joe looked stunned.

Susanna flashed him a smile. "Don't worry, you'll catch on." She pushed open a door at the end of the hall. On the other side was a big room lit by a ceiling fixture with bare bulbs. It had only two small high windows with bars on them. A couple of battered sofas, a dozen mismatched chairs, and a long scarred dining room table made the room look even shabbier. A counter at the far end held a beat-up coffee maker and paper cups.

"This is the greenroom," Susanna said. "It might have been pretty comfortable back in the days of vaudeville."

A young man who was slouched on one of the sofas, reading a magazine, looked up. "Hey, Susanna," he said. "Who's your friend?"

Susanna told him Joe's name and added, "He's joining the Irregulars, as of tonight. Orders from on high. Joe, meet Hector Arenas. He plays Charles, the fearless leader of the Irregulars. He'll give you the moves."

Hector stood up. He gave Joe the once-over, then asked, "Had much stage experience?"

"Well, I've been in some school plays," Joe said.

"Oh, terrific—a novice," Hector said. "Don't tell me . . . your sister's married to Hornby's cousin's hairdresser."

Joe folded his arms in front of his chest and gazed levelly at Hector. The guy obviously thought Joe had some connections that got him the role, and he seemed to resent it.

"Never mind," Hector said. "You don't have that much to do. You can't make things much worse than they are already."

He headed toward the door. "Come on, Joe," he said. "We'll let Martha, the wardrobe mistress, get a look at you. Then Susanna and I can show you what to do and when to do it. I hope you catch on fast. The curtain goes up in about five hours."

At seven-fifteen, Joe left the theater by the stage door and walked around to the front to meet his family. His brain was swirling with entrances, exits, lines, and cues. Would he remember it all? He hoped so. If the worst happened, he would simply watch Hector and do what he did.

Frank was already in front of the theater, along with a small crowd. His brown eyes scanned the theatergoers until he spotted Joe. Approaching his brother, Frank said, "You look wiped."

"You said it," Joe replied. "I don't know why they call these things plays. Being in one is hard work, not play. Where's everyone else?"

"Mom and Dad will be right along," Frank said. "Aunt Gertrude decided to stay home. She said she has better ways to spend an evening than to watch a play about rats."

"She's going to miss my off-Broadway debut?" Joe said. "I'm crushed!"

Frank chuckled and said, "So—did you get anywhere with the case?"

Joe said, "I think so. O'Lunny's right about the mood around here. Everyone's tense and nervous and expecting some kind of disaster. And Battenberg seems to be the focus of a lot of attention. He's the guy who plays Holmes. He acts as if he's suspicious of everybody. I don't know why yet. Maybe during the performance—"

Frank and Joe's parents hurried up just then. "Joe!" Laura Hardy exclaimed. "I can't believe that my own son is going to perform in a Broadway musical. But shouldn't you be backstage, getting into your costume?"

"I'm not on until the middle of the second act," Joe explained. "So I came out to be with you."

11

Fenton scanned the crowd filing through the doors, then looked at his wrist. "Why don't we take our seats?" he suggested. "We can talk inside."

As they crossed the lobby, Joe noticed a group of people leaving the auditorium with angry faces. Joe recognized Arnold Hausner, Bayport's deputy mayor. What had happened to make him so upset?

An usher took the Hardys' tickets and led them down the center aisle to Row L. Then she stopped abruptly, a confused look on her face. The row was full. She glanced at the tickets again, then studied them closely.

Turning to Fenton, the usher said, "I'm sorry, sir. Would you mind coming with me to the manager's office?"

"Is something wrong?" Fenton asked.

"Yes, sir," the usher replied. "I'm afraid so. Your tickets are duplicates. They're no good."

2 Backstage Battle

"What do you mean, our tickets are no good?" Frank said in amazement. "That's impossible!" People already seated were turning to stare. Frank had an impulse to pull his jacket up over his head, like some guy being arrested on the evening news.

Laura Hardy took Frank's arm and led him back up the aisle. "I'm sure your father can handle this," she said.

Joe and his father were right behind them. Fenton took his cue from his wife and said to the usher, "There must be some mistake. We're here as guests of Donald O'Lunny, the man who wrote the play. I can't believe that he would give us worthless tickets instead of house seats."

13

Joe knew that house seats were always available to friends of the actors and other people connected with a play.

"Yes, sir," the usher said, her face stony. Frank realized that the Hardys were not the only people who'd been given the wrong seats. The others with the angry faces who he'd seen leaving the auditorium had also had problems. No wonder the usher was so cold. She was in a terrible position. What could have happened?

"I'm sure the manager will clear this up," the usher said politely. "If you'll come with me, please?"

Fenton rolled his eyes. "Oh, well. Mistakes happen, I guess. Let's see if we can straighten this one out."

The Hardys followed the usher across the lobby. An unhappy crowd had gathered near the door to the manager's office. A man in a tuxedo stood with his back to the door. He was being bombarded with angry comments and questions. His forehead gleamed with sweat.

"This is an outrage," a stout man in a dark suit proclaimed. "Do you know who I am?"

"This is Judge Meagher," the young woman next to him said. "He was personally invited to the opening night by the producer, Mr. Hornby."

"I'm sure there's some explanation for the mix-

14

up," the man in the tuxedo said. Then, with obvious relief, he added, "Ah—here are Mr. Hornby and Mr. O'Lunny now. They'll clear this up."

The tall gray-haired man with O'Lunny eased through to the front of the crowd. Frank realized that he had to be Hornby, the producer.

Hornby held up his hands, palms outward. Slowly, the muttering died away. In a raised voice, he said, "I'd like to apologize to all of you. I'm sure you've heard this excuse before, but in this case there really does seem to have been a computer error."

A few people laughed sympathetically. Someone behind Frank muttered, "Yeah, sure. And the check's in the mail."

"We're doing everything we can to set matters straight," Hornby continued. "Our wonderfully gifted playwright, Donald O'Lunny, is here to tell you about that. Donald?"

O'Lunny looked and sounded flustered. "Yes, well . . ." he began. "We're holding the curtain while we try to sort this out. We hope that we have enough unsold seats to accommodate all of you. And in any case, you'll also receive complimentary tickets to a later performance."

The man behind Frank murmured, "If there is one."

"We'd also like to invite you all to join the company after the show for a champagne reception here in the lobby," O'Lunny concluded.

A look of surprise flashed across Hornby's face. The reception must have been a spur-of-the-moment idea by O'Lunny. Judging by the reaction of the crowd, it was a good one. Most of the angry looks faded, replaced by a chattering eagerness to see the show.

O'Lunny caught Frank's eye and nodded. Then he started moving toward the edge of the crowd.

"Come on," Frank whispered to Joe. They went up to O'Lunny, who took them by the elbows and led them to an empty corner of the lobby.

"This ticket business could have wrecked us," O'Lunny said in a low voice. "I don't believe it was an accident, either."

"We'll look into it," Frank promised. "But we can't do much until after the show."

"I realize that," O'Lunny replied. "What I'm afraid of is that this ticket foul-up is just the beginning. I have a strong feeling that something more—something worse—is going to happen."

He hesitated, looking down at the floor. "Frank, I hate to ask you to miss seeing the show, but will you come back with us now? Spend the evening behind the scenes? I know that Joe will be keeping an eye open, but he's going to be

16

pretty busy with his acting debut. I'd feel better knowing that both of you were on the spot."

"Sure, no problem," Frank said. He went off to tell his parents about the change of plans. Then he followed Joe and O'Lunny through an unmarked door. A long dimly lit corridor led backstage.

The area just off the stage was crowded with members of the cast and crew. Many of them were already in costume and makeup. Frank noticed the way their eyes shifted around. It made them seem more nervous than he would have expected, even for an opening night.

When the group noticed O'Lunny, the hum of conversation died away. O'Lunny gave them a wave and said, "Just a minor glitch, friends. Nothing to worry about. The curtain will go up in ten minutes or so. Oh—and there'll be a reception in the lobby after the show, with lots of nice bubbly. We might even manage to find some crackers and cheese."

The laughter that followed sounded warm and friendly. A little *too* warm and friendly, maybe? Frank found himself wondering how he and Joe were going to manage to read these people. After all, acting was their profession.

O'Lunny turned to Joe and Frank. In a low voice he said, "I'll be right back. Hold the fort." O'Lunny walked over to Li Wei, who looked

17

glamorous in a long black dress. Soon they were deep in conversation.

"Who's that?" Frank asked Joe.

"She's Li Wei, the composer," Joe replied. He looked around, then waved to Susanna, who was in white jeans and a T-shirt with a brightly colored parrot on it.

When she joined the Hardys, Joe said, "Susanna, this is my brother, Frank. He's O'Lunny's new assistant."

Susanna laughed. "You guys really do have pull, don't you? What, did your dad put a lot of money into the show?"

"Oh, something like that," Frank said.

"Well, good for him," Susanna said. "The way things are going, we Rats are going to need all the help we can get."

"What do you mean?" Frank asked. "Don't you think the show's any good?"

Susanna looked alarmed. "Don't even *say* things like that! It's a terrific show—good plot, great songs, and a wonderful cast. It'll make Broadway history . . . of one kind or another."

Frank was about to ask Susanna what she meant by her last comment when she added, "You'll have to excuse me. I need to get in some meditation time before I go on."

She didn't wait for a response before walking

away. "Wait till Dad hears that he's become a big Broadway angel," Joe said as he watched her go.

"He can handle it," Frank said, grinning.

A man with a clipboard under his arm walked by, calmly giving directions to the cast: "Places, please. Places for opening curtain. Places, please."

"We'd better get out of the way," Joe said as the actors moved toward the stage.

The lights came up on the set, but the curtain was still closed. From the wing, where Frank was standing, he could see the gloomy sinister warehouse set facing the audience. The stone walls of the set oozed with moisture. He could almost smell the fungus growing in long-neglected corners. He could also see the backs of the stone walls. They were nothing more than flats, tall rectangular wooden frames covered with painted canvas. On the back of the one nearest him someone had spray-painted, *Act I Scene 1.*

From the other side of the curtain came a burst of applause, followed by the muffled sound of music. A tall broad-shouldered man in an old-fashioned knee-length coat brushed past Frank and Joe. He was wearing a shiny top hat and carrying a gold-headed walking stick.

"That must be the Giant Rat," Joe whispered. "I'll fill you in on the plot later."

The man took his position in the middle of a half dozen villainous-looking gang members and put one hand out as if he were making a speech. The curtains slid open, and the audience burst into applause. The actors waited for the clapping to die down, then started to sing and move. Led by the Giant Rat, each verse of their song started as a menacing rumble and gradually built to a rousing shout of "*Rats* in every alley!" The audience loved it.

In the scene that followed, Frank learned that the Giant Rat and his gang were plotting to disrupt a royal wedding. This would distract the detectives of Scotland Yard while the Rats carried out a series of crimes throughout London.

One of the gang had an objection. Their plot might fool Scotland Yard, but what about the great and dreaded detective, Sherlock Holmes? What if he caught on?

The Giant Rat gave an evil chuckle. "Holmes?" he said. "Don't worry. I have a plan to take care of him!"

The scene ended and the curtain closed. To make room for the stage crew as they rapidly switched the set, Frank and Joe pressed themselves back against the wall behind them. Before their eyes, the set was transformed into a Victorian living room, complete with fireplace and overstuffed furniture. Frank thought it looked like a faithful reproduction of 221B Baker Street, Sherlock Holmes's famous address.

"That's Holmes and Watson," Joe whispered, as the actors walked out onstage. "And Mrs. Hudson, the housekeeper."

Frank grinned. "I'd already deduced that," he said. "Elementary, my dear Joseph."

"I'll see you later," Joe added. "I'd better get back to the dressing room. Wait till you hear this next song. Believe it or not, it's about having fish for breakfast. Yuck!"

Joe left. A couple of minutes later, the curtains opened again. Frank liked the number, "Kippers and Eggs" and thought the actor playing Holmes was exactly right—sharp as a tack, a little scornful of others, yet secretly hungry for their applause.

Frank's favorite moment came when Holmes noticed an ink spot on Watson's finger and a trace of mud on his pants cuff. From these minor clues, Holmes constructed a whole series of brilliant deductions. But then, after he explained his reasoning, Watson sniffed and said that it had really been very simple after all.

Frank had to smile ruefully. In solving their cases, he and Joe had encountered people who acted that way more than once. After a mystery was solved, it didn't seem so complicated anymore.

As the scene continued, Frank reminded himself that he wasn't there simply to enjoy the play. He roamed from spot to spot, trying to seem casual. He studied the people backstage as well as onstage, the sets, equipment, and the building itself. It was important to know how everything looked ordinarily. Otherwise, he might not realize that something was unusual.

Onstage, Holmes and Watson's breakfast was interrupted by a man in a mask who begged Holmes for help. Holmes spotted the coat of arms on the man's signet ring and instantly recognized him as a duke, a cousin of the Queen. He agreed to keep His Grace's identity secret and pledged to do whatever he could to foil the Giant Rat's plot.

The duke thanked him and left. Holmes stood for a moment, chin in hand, deep in thought. Then he donned his deerstalker cap and caped overcoat, thrust a revolver in his pocket, and exclaimed, "Come, Watson! The game's afoot!"

The curtain closed to applause and cheers.

Holmes came striding offstage, directly toward Frank. Frank had to remind himself that the man wasn't really Sherlock Holmes. He was an actor named—what was it?—Battenberg.

Frank was about to congratulate Battenberg on his performance when the actor pointed his finger at one of the stagehands, whose name was

Bill. "You there," Battenberg said in a clipped voice. "I want to speak to you."

"Who, me?" the stagehand said. He looked puzzled.

"That's right," Battenberg said. "My entrance at the beginning of this scene—you were in my way. You will please make very sure that it doesn't happen again."

The stagehand said, "Sorry, but we've got to shift the Scene One set offstage, and we're tight for time. Can't you just step around me?"

Battenberg gave him a cold look. "My good fellow, you apparently have not noticed that I am the star of this show. You should be asking yourself how to make things easier for me, not going out of your way to inconvenience me."

The actor who was playing Watson stepped forward and said, "Now, Charles, the crew have their own jobs to do."

"Don't you 'Now, Charles' me, Gordean," Battenberg retorted. "I am well aware of your agenda. You want me out of the way, so that your friend Will Robertson can step into the part. Hornby may have talked me into accepting him as my understudy, but, I promise you, that's as far as it goes. I am *never* going to let him take over my role. He'll play Holmes over my dead body. Is that clear?"

23

Somebody touched Frank's shoulder and murmured, "What's all the uproar?"

Frank glanced sideways. A ragged dirty-faced London street kid was standing next to him. Frank looked again and recognized Joe. "Battenberg got mad at a stagehand," Frank explained in an undertone. "Gordean tried to calm him down, so now Battenberg's mad at him instead."

Joe said, "It figures. Battenberg's been like a firecracker with a short fuse all afternoon. Too bad he's so good in the Sherlock Holmes role. Otherwise, maybe they'd dump him."

"Does everybody in the show feel that way?" Frank asked.

"Everybody *I've* talked to," Joe replied. "They all seem to think he's a good actor, but a rotten human being. So far I haven't seen any reason to doubt them."

Frank turned his attention back to Gordean and Battenberg, who were still arguing. Several cast and crew members were also observing the confrontation.

"It's a waste of breath, trying to reason with you," Gordean said. He turned on his heel and stalked away.

Battenberg watched him go. Then he glared at the little circle of spectators and said, "I'm sure you all have better things to do than stand here with your mouths open."

24

The onlookers began to drift away. Frank took a step backward, then frowned. He had a sudden impression that the floor was tilting. That was impossible. Still, *something* was wrong.

He looked up, then grabbed Joe's arm. "The flat," he gasped. "It's falling. And Battenberg's in front of it!"

3 Set to Fall

"Look out!" Joe shouted, as the flat toppled forward. "Heads up!"

He dashed forward and grabbed Battenberg by the arm. Battenberg struggled, unaware of the danger at first, but then he acquiesced. Joe dragged him to safety.

Frank and two of the actors had caught the flat by the edges. They were holding it up, keeping it from hitting the floor. Frank's face was red from the strain.

Two stagehands rushed over. "Okay," one of them said. "We've got it." They grasped the sides of the flat and carefully raised it back to the vertical.

"Release me, young man," a voice said, close to Joe's ear.

Startled, Joe realized he was still gripping Battenberg's arm. He let go and took a step backward. "Are you okay?" he asked the actor.

Battenberg brushed off his sleeve. "Of course I am," he said. "It was quite unnecessary to manhandle me like that. I'm still capable of moving on my own, thank you."

What a grouch! Joe thought. Aloud, he said, "You're welcome. Anytime."

Battenberg sniffed and looked around. Then he raised his voice and said, "I'd like your attention."

When the group fell silent, Battenberg announced, "What just happened—or almost happened—was no accident. It was certainly part of a plot aimed at injuring me, and through me, the play."

Celia Hatteras, the gray-haired woman playing Mrs. Hudson, said, "Charles, dear, what a terrible thing to say."

In a dramatic voice, Battenberg replied, "Terrible, yes. But nonetheless true. However, the plotters have chosen the wrong target. I am not going to wait idly by while they mount their vile attacks."

Raising his right arm level with his shoulder so

27

that his cape opened with a flourish, Battenberg made a slow sweeping gesture that took in everyone around him. "Let the villains heed this," he continued. "I intend to conduct an investigation. I mean to unmask those who conspire against me and see they get the punishment they deserve. And no threats, no cowardly attacks, will deter me."

As Battenberg fell silent, somebody near Joe muttered sarcastically, "Curtain. Ovation. Film at eleven."

Hornby, the producer-director, hurried up. He looked tired and harried. "Is this a performance or a cocktail party?" he demanded. "Come on, people, get ready for Act Two. The first act went swimmingly. Let's keep that energy flowing."

Battenberg walked off through the crowd with his head held high, his cape billowing behind him. He didn't look to either side. The other actors began to drift off.

Joe looked around. Frank was standing next to the flat, talking to one of the stagehands. Joe joined them.

"So tell me, Bill—what usually keeps one of these things from falling over?" Frank asked.

The stagehand pointed to three triangular wooden braces attached to the back of the flat. "See those?" he said. "They rest on the floor,

28

sort of like table legs. Then we put sandbags across the bottom struts. The weight of the bags keeps the flat from falling over, but we can still move it easily when we need to."

Joe looked around. "Sandbags like those?" he asked, pointing to a shadowy corner.

"That's right," Bill replied. "But I don't know what they're doing over there. They should have been on top of the struts of the flat that fell over, not piled in the corner."

"Maybe somebody moved them," Frank said. "You didn't notice anybody hanging around there, did you?"

Bill shrugged. "Nope. I wasn't paying attention, though. Like everybody else, I was watching the shindy between Sherlock Holmes and Dr. Watson . . . I mean, Battenberg and Gordean."

Frank cleared his throat and said, "You know, Bill, I thought Battenberg was out of line, picking on you the way he did when he came offstage just now."

"I don't let it bother me," Bill said with another shrug. "He's got a rep for that kind of stuff."

"I don't know . . . if somebody treated me badly, I might think about teaching him a lesson," Frank said.

Bill's face tightened. "Now just hold on," he

said. "I didn't fiddle with that flat. If I wanted to get back at somebody—you'll notice I said *if*—you know what I'd do? I'd fill a plastic bag with flour, take it up into the flies, and bombs away!"

Joe grinned. "I'll keep that in mind, in case a sack of flour lands on me. But you know, Bill—seriously—those sandbags didn't move by themselves. Somebody around here has got a mean sense of humor. I think we'd all better keep our eyes open."

"I guess that's right," Bill said, nodding slowly. He looked past Frank's shoulder. Joe noticed a second stagehand who was motioning to Bill. "I have to go finish setting up for Act Two," Bill said.

"What do you think?" Frank asked in an undertone, as Bill walked away.

Joe thought for a moment. "Anybody could have shifted those sandbags," he said. "You could do it with your foot, in three seconds. And like Bill, everybody was watching the argument between Battenberg and Gordean. But how could anyone be sure that Battenberg would be the only one in the way of the flat?"

"Good point," Frank said, nodding. "I know it looks like Battenberg was the target. And he himself is convinced of it. But what if he wasn't? Maybe whoever did it didn't care who got hit."

"You mean the real target was the show itself," Joe said. "That would fit with that mix-up over the tickets. But who'd want to wreck the show?"

"Somebody who doesn't want *The Giant Rat of Sumatra* to be a hit," Frank replied.

Joe shook his head. "But, Frank, that eliminates everybody backstage. We all want the show to be a success—O'Lunny, Hornby, all of us in the cast, even the stage crew."

Frank grinned. " 'All of *us* in the cast'?" he repeated. "Hey, don't forget *why* you're playing that part."

Joe could feel his face reddening under his makeup. "All I meant was—" he started to say.

"I know what you meant," Frank said. "And that's a good point you made. But what if you're not the only one who's playing a double role? Somebody could be pretending to be a loyal member of the company but secretly be working for an enemy."

"Then how do we catch him . . . or her?"

"For now, we keep a close watch on everyone," Frank replied. "And we wait for our 'villain,' as Battenberg put it, to make a mistake. Hey, shouldn't you be getting ready? The intermission must be just about over."

Joe gulped. "You're right," he said. "I'd better run. Wish me luck."

31

Joe hurried down the hallway that led to the men's dressing room. Frank watched him for a moment. Then he walked around behind the flat that had fallen. The braces in back were in deep shadow. The flat itself blocked most of the light from the stage.

Frank got down on one knee. There was a sandbag draped across the bottom strut of the nearest brace. He reached out and grabbed it. Then he looked over his shoulder. There were several actors and stagehands moving around the flats for Act Two, not far away. Not one of them seemed to notice him, crouched in the shadows.

Frank stood up and walked to the edge of the stage. He saw that the person who had moved the sandbags hadn't been taking such a big risk. Everyone had been paying attention to the argument between Battenberg and Gordean at the time the contrast between the brightly lit stage and the pool of shadow at the rear of the flat would have made it hard to notice anything.

"Frank! Thank goodness!" O'Lunny came rushing over and grabbed Frank's sleeve. "I just heard that Charles was almost hit by a piece of falling scenery, and that you and Joe saved him from a broken neck."

"That's somewhat exaggerated," Frank said. "Joe pulled him out of the way, sure. But the flat

32

wasn't *that* heavy. If it had hit Battenberg, he might have sprained his wrist or twisted a knee, but I don't think it could have broken his neck."

O'Lunny said, "All right, be modest. I'm grateful just the same. I'd better speak to Bettina, our stage manager. She's going to have to see to it that everyone in the crew is more careful."

"We don't think it was the crew's oversight," Frank told him. "It looks as though somebody deliberately took the weights off the braces and then gave the flat a push."

O'Lunny's eyes widened. "But that's dangerous," he said. "It was just luck that nobody was hurt. And next time we might not be so lucky."

"Weren't you expecting something like this?" Frank asked him.

O'Lunny rubbed his forehead. "Oh, I don't know what I was expecting," he said in a tired voice. "Trouble of some sort, yes. But dangerous pranks? I thought we were too much of a family for that sort of thing."

"Can you think of anyone who might want *The Giant Rat* to fail?" Frank asked. "Want it badly enough to do something about it?"

"No," O'Lunny said promptly. "Look, Frank, the theater isn't the kind of cutthroat business you seem to think it is. If somebody else has a bigger success than me, I may eat my heart out, but I wouldn't dream of trying to undermine him or her. Why should I? Anytime a play or musical hits it big on Broadway, it gets more people into the habit of going to the theater. And that means that the next time I put on a play, there's a bigger potential audience. In the long run, one person's success is good for all of us."

"Then who messed with the tickets, and who pushed over that flat?" Frank asked.

"I don't know, Frank," O'Lunny said. "I'm hoping you and Joe can find out. But maybe we're on a wild goose chase. Maybe those duplicate tickets really were caused by a computer foul-up, and someone was careless with the sandbags."

He glanced across the stage and added, "I'd better go. The next act is starting. Good luck, Frank. We're all counting on you. I'll come find you after the show."

Frank found a spot between two of the side curtains where he could watch both the stage and the area just offstage. The setting for this scene was a sinister back street near the London docks, late at night. In the background, the funnels of a steamship loomed over the roofs of a row of dirty, shabby tenements. Wisps of fog drifted onstage from a machine in the wings.

"Quiet, please," the stage manager said as the lights dimmed. "Curtain going up."

A tense silence fell. To Frank it felt as if all the people backstage and in the audience were holding their breath.

As the curtain started to slide open, Frank heard a low voice growl, "This show will never make it to Broadway. I'll see to that."

4 The Sign of the Hanged Man

Frank spun around, then froze in place, his eyes probing the darkness. He felt like a scout on night patrol in enemy territory. Where was the person who had spoken? Who was he talking to? And whoever he was, why was he so determined to wreck the show?

Frank held his breath and listened intently. But if the speaker or his companion said anything more, it was covered by a burst of applause from the auditorium.

He heard a noise somewhere nearby. It sounded like a shoe scraping the irregular wooden floor. Moving silently, Frank went toward the sound. After two steps, he bumped into a thick

36

green velvet curtain. The dust on it made him want to sneeze.

Feeling his way, Frank edged around the curtain. A few feet from him, the dim form of someone was hurrying away. He started to follow.

Something—a faint sound, a movement of air—alerted him. He started to turn, to face whatever new danger threatened. As he did, he went into a defensive crouch and raised his hands to guard position.

Too late. He was still in the middle of his turn when something heavy slammed him at the base of his skull, just below and behind the left ear. A gray fog spread across his vision, shot through with flashes of lightning. His eyes rolled upward, and he felt himself slumping to the floor.

Hang on! Frank ordered himself, as he sprawled out flat. Don't pass out! He focused on counting silently to twenty-five. By the time he reached twenty-one, he was able to push himself up into a sitting position. At twenty-five, he used the green velvet curtain to pull himself to his feet.

His left foot bumped into something on the floor. Frank waited while a dizzy spell passed. Then he bent down and felt the object with his fingertips. He knew at once what it was—one of the sandbags. Perfect for hitting somebody over the head without making a noise.

Frank had a dim memory that, after slugging him, his assailant had gone toward the dressing rooms. He started in that direction. But he hadn't yet recovered as fully as he thought. After three steps, he felt himself losing his balance. He staggered sideways. His hip bumped into a table. The objects on the table rattled loudly.

"Hey, you!" a man said in an angry whisper. A hand grabbed Frank's left arm.

Frank spun around, freeing his arm, and started to throw a counterpunch. Just in time he realized that the other man wasn't attacking him.

"Who are you? What are you doing here?" the man demanded.

By now Frank's eyes had adjusted to the dim lighting. The guy who was talking to him was tall and thin, with a hawklike face. He was a member of the Giant Rat's gang.

Frank identified himself and added, "I'm Donald O'Lunny's assistant."

"Oh. Well, you'd better be more careful if you want to stay backstage," the man said. "Keep quiet and out of the way. We have a play to put on."

Another Rat came over and murmured, "Come on, Will. We're on."

The two actors moved quickly toward the

stage. Frank thought for a moment. Will? Then he remembered. The man who had just been scolding him had to be Will Robertson, Battenberg's understudy in the role of Holmes. In other words, a guy who would go from being a member of the chorus to being the star of the show . . . *if* something happened to Battenberg.

The scene in the street ended. Frank stared, wide-eyed. In the half darkness, the whole set seemed to change shape and position. After watching for a moment, Frank realized that it was starting to revolve. The floor of the stage was a gigantic turntable.

Within seconds the street, the buildings, the lampposts, and the carriages all vanished from sight. In their place was the interior of a vast shadowy warehouse. Rickety uneven stairs led to a barely glimpsed upper level. Ropes and cargo nets dangled from rusty iron beams. It looked almost like the set from the opening of the play, but it had been subtly distorted to seem even more sinister.

The Rats were sitting around a battered table. While the Giant Rat stirred them up with a song about the crimes they were planning, Susanna, off to the side and facing away from them, sang a harmonizing ballad about wanting a quiet life of peace and love. The two merged songs were followed by a roar of clapping and even cheers and whistling from the audience.

O'Lunny came over and stood next to Frank. "A great moment," he said quietly. "Li Wei has outdone herself. This is only the second show she's composed, and she's got a bright future if this makes it to Broadway and is a hit."

Frank glanced over at O'Lunny. He looked not so much proud as moved. Frank had the feeling that O'Lunny barely remembered that the scene and the words to the duet were his work. He was simply appreciating them for what they were and giving Li Wei the credit.

"I think you've got a hit here," Frank said. "The songs are great, the sets are terrific, the acting is first-rate."

"We've got a hit—*if* nothing goes wrong," O'Lunny retorted. "Show business is full of *ifs*. And we've got more than our share of them."

Frank thought of repeating what he had overheard before he'd been slugged. But what was the point? O'Lunny was already convinced that someone was out to wreck the show. He didn't need further proof. Especially if hearing it might ruin what ought to be a triumphant night for him.

"Your brother's first scene is coming up," O'Lunny added.

The turntable revolved again. Now the cast was in Baker Street, outside Holmes's home.

Unlike the East End street scene, this upper-middle-class neighborhood was bright, clean, and cheerful. Most of the windows were decorated with flower boxes filled with geraniums, petunias, and other bright blossoms.

On the sidewalk, half a dozen "boys," the Baker Street Irregulars, in ragged but neat outfits, were playing a game of pitch-penny. Hector was the leader. Frank had to look twice to spot Joe under his makeup.

Holmes appeared center-stage, and the boys clustered around him. Looking stern, Holmes declared, "Detection is, or ought to be, an exact science." The boys nodded. He went on to say that the case of the Giant Rat of Sumatra was vitally important to the kingdom, and that he was counting on them to keep a careful watch on the Giant Rat and his gang. "You must be clever and never let them out of your sight." The Baker Street Irregulars tossed their caps in the air and shouted, "Hip, hip, hoorah!" Then they sang a chorus with a marching rhythm about being "regular Irregulars." Joe marched around the stage like a professional.

For the rest of the play, Frank continued to wander around backstage, watching for anything suspicious. Nothing struck him, though.

After the grand finale, in which Holmes, Watson, the Baker Street Irregulars, and the cause of

Justice triumphed over the evil Giant Rat and his band of cutthroats, the cast took one curtain call after another. When they filed offstage after the last one, their faces were glowing with pride.

"You were all wonderful," O'Lunny called to them. "Don't forget, bubbly in the lobby."

"Is that the title of your next hit?" someone called out. O'Lunny laughed.

Frank spotted Joe in the crowd and went over to him. "Great job," he said, grinning. "You didn't trip once."

"I'm saving that for tomorrow night," Joe replied. "How did it go backstage?"

"Funny you should ask." Frank quickly told him about being attacked near the green velvet curtain. "I know Will Robertson was close by, but that doesn't prove he did it."

"Maybe the opposite," Joe said. "If I'd just slugged you, I think I'd try to get away from the scene of the crime as fast as I could. Speaking of getting away, I'd better go change and remove this makeup. Mom and Dad are expecting to see us at the reception."

Frank waited for Joe outside the dressing room. The cast members were quick-change artists. Most of them came out of the dressing room long before Joe did. Finally, he came out in his regular clothes, and the two Hardys made their way to the front of the theater.

The lobby was crowded with actors, crew members, and playgoers. Frank and Joe helped themselves to some potato chips and mineral water with lemon slices. Then they positioned themselves where they could see the entire lobby and looked over the scene.

Battenberg was standing at the foot of the grand staircase, surrounded by a half circle of admirers. Not far away, Gordean, who played Watson, watched Battenberg with a mocking look on his face. Battenberg saw him and glared. Gilbert Hornby, the producer, hurried over, took Gordean by the arm, and started talking earnestly to him.

In an undertone, Joe said, "If anything more happens to Battenberg, I know who my main suspect will be."

"But Gordean couldn't have knocked over that flat," Frank pointed out. "He was right in the middle of his argument with Battenberg when it fell over."

"Yeah, but what about his friend Robertson?" Joe replied. "I wouldn't mind knowing where *he* was at the time."

Laura and Fenton Hardy waved from the other side of the room; Joe and Frank forged through the crowd to join them.

"You were terrific," Laura said to Joe, giving him a hug.

43

After a round of handshakes and congratulations, Fenton said in a low voice, "Any developments?"

"A few," Joe replied. "We'll fill you in when we get home."

"Don't be too late," his father said. "I've got an early flight tomorrow. I'll want to get to bed at a decent hour."

"If either of us can sleep, after the excitement of watching Joe on stage," Laura said. "I hardly recognized you in your makeup and costume. But you looked very handsome."

Joe shrugged and looked at the floor. Frank knew he was trying to hide how pleased he was at the compliment.

"I'm afraid we should be getting home," Laura continued. "Your father still has to pack."

When their parents left, Frank and Joe separated to mingle with the crowd. After about fifteen minutes, they rejoined each other.

"This is a waste of time," Joe declared. "Everyone's on best behavior. Let's find O'Lunny. Maybe he can let us into the office. We can take a shot at hacking the computer and finding out what happened with all those tickets."

They scanned the crowd, but O'Lunny wasn't in sight. In fact, practically everyone from the

44

show had gone. The members of the audience were left to chat with each other.

"Maybe O'Lunny's backstage," Frank suggested. He led Joe down the corridor they had taken earlier. It was even gloomier and more deserted than before. Except for a few dim work lights and the lamp on the watchman's desk, darkness pooled everywhere. In the silence, every distant creak of a rafter or joist sounded as loud as a gunshot.

They walked out onto the stage and began to circle it, looking for anything unusual. Frank found it a spooky experience. The set seemed to loom over them, to tilt inward, to want to crush them.

Suddenly Joe stopped and grabbed Frank's sleeve. "They didn't have graffiti in Victorian London, did they?" Joe asked.

"I don't think so," Frank said. "Why?"

Joe pointed up at the nearest wall.

Even in the dim light, Frank could make out the spray painting of a stick figure with a Holmes-type deerstalker cap on its head. Frank took a step closer. A hangman's noose was around the figure's neck. Under the picture was written the following:

The Real Rat Will Die!

45

5 The Dangling Clue

Frank studied the sketch of the hanged man and the words under it. Then he leaned closer to the wall and sniffed.

"The spray paint's fresh," he said. "I can still smell it."

Joe took a sniff of his own and said, "You're right. So whoever did it is either still around or must have left just a few minutes ago."

"I wonder if—" Frank started to say. He broke off as a powerful flashlight beam swept the stage and stopped, focusing on him and Joe.

"Hey there, you two," came a gruff voice. "What are you up to?"

"I'm in the cast," Joe said quickly.

"And I'm Mr. O'Lunny's assistant," Frank added.

The flashlight drew closer. Squinting and looking past it, Frank could make out a man with a white mustache and sideburns, wearing a uniform of some kind. He was probably a security guard.

"Mr. O'Lunny's assistant?" the man said. "Then how come I've never seen either of you before?"

The beam of light moved a little upward, lighting the drawing on the wall. "So that's it," the man said. "Vandalism. Don't move—I'm going to call the police."

Frank said, "Now, wait a minute, Mr. . . . ?"

"Gonsalves. Tomas Gonsalves," the man said. "I'm the watchman here."

"Mr. Gonsalves," Frank resumed, "why don't you ask Donald O'Lunny about us? He'll tell you that we're not up to anything."

"Or the producer, Mr. Hornby," Joe added. "He knows about us."

Gonsalves let out an amused snort and said, "They're both gone for the night. No, I'd better call a friend of mine, Officer Riley. He'll take care of you."

"We know Con Riley," Frank said, deliberately using the Bayport police officer's first name. "Go ahead and call him. He'll vouch for us."

47

The light wavered. Was the watchman suddenly a little less sure of himself?

Suddenly, from the back of the auditorium, a voice called, "What's going on up there? Tomas, is that you?"

"That sounds like O'Lunny," Joe muttered to Frank.

"Yes, sir," Gonsalves called back. "Would you come up here? I need some advice."

Moments later O'Lunny joined them onstage. He was wearing his raincoat and carrying a battered briefcase.

"Do you know these fellows?" Gonsalves asked O'Lunny.

"This one—Frank—is my new assistant, and the other is his brother. He's an actor. They're all right."

O'Lunny then switched on the stage work lights. After looking over the stick figure, he shook his head and said, "I'd better get one of the scene painters over here first thing in the morning. We don't want to upset the cast."

Frank turned to Gonsalves, "Do you know if there are any clean plastic bags somewhere?"

"I keep some in my desk," the watchman replied. "The small size. I use them to store lost objects that turn up."

Frank followed Gonsalves over to the desk next to the stage door. While Gonsalves hunted for

48

the plastic bags, Frank noticed a sign-out sheet on a clipboard lying on the desk. The last two names on the list were Ewan Gordean and Will Robertson. They had left less than half an hour ago.

Gonsalves noticed Frank's interest and said, "That's not complete. Some people left by the front and didn't sign out. Is one bag enough?"

"Two or three, if you can spare them," Frank replied. He took the bags and rejoined Joe and O'Lunny. With his pocketknife, he carefully scraped some of the white paint into one of the bags, then sealed it.

"Those spray cans spatter a lot," Frank explained to O'Lunny. "We'll be watching for specks of white paint on people's clothes. If we find them, we'll be able to compare the chemical composition of the spots with the graffiti."

"Yes, I see," O'Lunny said. "What I don't see is how you're going to scrape paint spots off someone's clothes without being noticed."

Joe grinned and said, "We'll manage. One handy thing about actors is that they change into costumes and leave their own clothes behind in the dressing room."

"By the way," Frank said, "can you let us into the office? We'd like to try solving the mystery of those duplicate tickets."

"Of course," O'Lunny replied. "Come with

me. I'll just warn Tomas that you'll be in there. We don't want him trying to arrest you a second time in one night."

The Hardys followed O'Lunny to an unmarked door next to the costume room and waited while he unlocked it.

The cubicle on the other side of the door was just big enough for a couple of chairs, a filing cabinet, and a desk that held a computer, a telephone, and an answering machine.

"This is just makeshift, of course," O'Lunny explained. "We took over this room for the duration of our run in Bayport. The real office is in New York. Do you know how to operate this sort of computer? It's pretty old-fashioned, I'm afraid."

"Sure," Joe said, sitting down at the keyboard. He booted up, waited for the memory check to finish, and called up a directory of files on the hard disk. "I'll need the password," he added.

"I'm afraid I don't know it," O'Lunny said. "I never use this machine. Maybe it's written down somewhere."

Frank looked through each drawer of the desk, then took the drawer out to check behind it. Joe turned over the keyboard and the mouse pad. No luck.

O'Lunny looked at his watch and said, "Listen,

fellows, I have to go. First thing tomorrow, I'll get the password from Mila—the woman who manages the office—and let you know what it is."

"We'll stay a little longer," Joe said. "There are still a few tricks we can try."

After the door had closed behind O'Lunny, Frank turned to Joe and said, "What kinds of tricks? Punching in groups of random letters and hoping one of them works? I'd rather invest my savings in lottery tickets. The odds are better."

"The reason most people write down their computer passwords is because they're afraid they'll forget them," Joe said.

Frank rolled his eyes. "No, *duh!* So?"

Joe smiled. "So if they don't write it down, it's because they're *not* afraid of forgetting it. In other words, it's something obvious."

"Brilliant theory, Joe," Frank said, "but I'm going to need proof."

"Simple," Joe said. He turned to the computer and clicked on a directory. A box appeared on the screen, demanding the password. He typed something and hit Return. Nothing happened. He typed again. Still nothing. He scratched his neck a moment, then made a third try.

The box disappeared, replaced by a list of files.

"Bingo!" Joe exclaimed.

"That's the password? Bingo?" Frank asked.

"Don't be ridiculous," Joe replied. "First I tried *Sumatra*. I didn't bother with *Rat* because it's too short. Then I tried *Holmes*. And when that didn't work, I tried—"

"Sherlock!" Frank said. "My brother, the genius," he added.

Joe feinted a left to Frank's midsection. Frank blocked it.

Turning back to the screen, Joe studied it. "Let's see . . . CONTRCTS, SUPPLIER, BROAD-WAY, INSURNCE . . . It sure would be easier if these names could have more than eight letters in them. Okay, here we go—COMPTIX."

The subdirectory contained a database file, with the names and addresses of people who were supposed to get complimentary tickets, and a program in BASIC to generate and send the tickets. Joe opened the program. Then he and Frank got down to the demanding task of working out exactly what the program did.

After twenty minutes hunched over the screen, Frank straightened up. Pointing to one set of commands, he said, "Look, Joe. So far the program selected unsold seats, printed tickets for them, assigned the seats to people on the comp list, and printed cover letters."

"That all sounds okay," Joe said.

Frank nodded. "Right. But now these lines of code here send a message back to the ticket-sales program saying that those seats are still unsold. So the computer goes right ahead and sells them again. No wonder there were already people in those places when the VIPs showed up!"

"I guess you're right," Joe said. "But wait a minute. Couldn't it just be a dumb mistake? After all, the seats *weren't* sold. They'd been given away."

"Possible," Frank conceded. "Unlikely, though. An earlier subroutine had already marked the places as unavailable. Why go back and change that . . . unless you were deliberately setting out to create a mess?"

Joe said, "I see your point. So our trickster is somebody who has access to this computer, who knows the password, and who can program in BASIC, which isn't as common as it used to be a few years ago. It shouldn't be hard to figure out who it is, just by a process of elimination."

"That's what worries me," Frank replied. "It looks a little *too* easy. I can't believe our bad guy is that careless. I've got a feeling that we still have a few surprises in store for us."

After breakfast the next morning, Joe and Frank drove downtown to the Orpheum. They parked the car in a lot and walked back to the theater. The stage door was unlocked. No one was at the watchman's desk.

53

"Not the greatest security," Joe remarked. "Anybody could walk into this place and do anything he wanted."

They walked down the hall to the office. The door wasn't locked, but the room was empty. On the screen of the computer, rows of pink pigs with wings flew slowly from one side to the other.

"Hi," a voice said from behind them. "Can I help you?"

Joe and Frank turned. The speaker was a young woman with a long dark brown ponytail and striking blue eyes. She was wearing jeans and a purple knit shirt, and she had a ballpoint pen tucked behind her left ear. Joe thought she looked like a college student . . . probably a theater major.

Joe introduced himself and Frank.

"Oh, sure, I heard about you guys," she said. "I'm Mila. I'm sort of in charge of the office."

"That sounds like a big job," Frank said. "You handle the accounts and ticket sales and everything, all by yourself?"

Mila laughed. "I may be great, but I'm not *that* great! The box office is a separate operation, and so is payroll and so on. What I handle here is stuff like rehearsal schedules, promotion, and business. Anyway, what can I do for you?"

"Did you hear about the mix-up with the

complimentary tickets last night?" Frank asked. "Mr. O'Lunny asked me to find out how it happened. What was it, some sort of computer error?"

Mila's face fell. "I wish I knew," she said. "I use the computer all the time. But whenever something messes up, I have to shout for help. Luckily, one of the cast member's an expert."

Keeping his voice casual, Joe asked, "Oh? Who's that?"

"Hector Arenas," Mila replied. "When he's between roles, he works as a programmer."

"Hector? The guy who plays the leader of the Irregulars," Joe asked. "The one Susanna is supposed to be in love with?"

Mila nodded.

Before Joe and Frank could ask any more questions, Hornby arrived. He looked at the Hardys in surprise, his eyes bloodshot with circles under them, but he didn't say anything. He set his briefcase on the table and pulled a roll of antacid tablets from his pocket. After chewing one, he said, "Mila, there are a few details I need to go over with you. Will you fellows excuse us?"

"Sure. See you later," Joe said. As he and Frank walked down the hall, he added in an undertone, "So Hector's a professional programmer. And if he helps Mila with the computer, it's a good bet that he knows the password."

Frank frowned. "I know. We should be careful not to jump to conclusions, but it looks as if we'd better keep a close eye on Hector."

Twenty minutes later rehearsals started. Joe and Frank watched from the wings. Hector was standing half a dozen feet away, waiting for his entrance cue. Susanna was onstage alone.

The rehearsal pianist played the introductory passage to Susanna's song. Susanna took a deep breath and opened her mouth. Joe knew the verses well, and waited for the first line.

But what came out instead was a horrified scream.

When Joe saw what had terrorized Susanna, his stomach twisted into a knot. The tweed-clad body of Sherlock Holmes was plummeting toward the stage. It jerked to a stop, then swayed in midair. A hangman's noose was pulled tightly around its neck, and the head dangled lifelessly.

6 Danger in the Fog

Frozen in fear, Susanna stared up at the body, the blood drained from her face. Frank and Joe immediately sprinted out onto the stage.

Hector was ahead of them. He reached Susanna, put his arm around her shoulders, and walked her away from the awful sight.

Hornby came running out from the wings. Over the confused shouts and screams, the producer called out, "It's all right! It's only a dummy!"

Frank stared up. Under the deerstalker cap, facial features were merely sketched on flesh-colored cloth. But the rest—the body, arms, and legs—still looked convincing.

More and more people came crowding out onto

57

the stage. Most of them stood gaping in disbelief. Hornby, looking irritated, turned toward the wings. "Bettina, get that thing down, will you?" he shouted to the stage manager, a woman with short blond hair. A moment later one of the stagehands went scampering up a ladder to the catwalk.

The dummy started to descend slowly. Frank moved closer, ready to help catch it. Joe was next to him. The dummy's feet were almost level with Frank's head before he spotted a thin transparent line tied to one of the ankles.

Joe saw it, too. "Monofilament fish line," he murmured. "It's made of nylon—thin, strong, and practically invisible. I used some a couple of months ago to hang a picture."

Frank reached up and caught the line in his hand. From the dummy's leg, it stretched toward the side of the stage at just above head height. Keeping his hand closed around it, Frank followed it across the stage. The other end was tied to a pipe offstage.

"What are you doing, Frank?" It was O'Lunny, looking more worried than ever.

Frank showed him the nylon line. "All our joker had to do was give it a yank, and that dummy came tumbling down," he explained. "But where did he get the dummy in the first place?"

"It's from a scene we cut in rehearsal," O'Lunny said. "We decided that having a body dangle over the stage on a rope was a cheap effect. Obviously, somebody doesn't mind cheap effects."

Frank looked around. "Whoever did it had to be somewhere under the fishing line at the right moment," he said. "But it wouldn't have taken more than a couple of seconds to reach up and pull the line. What gets me mad is that Joe and I were standing just a few feet away. But we were watching Susanna. I don't know why I can't remember who was standing in this area. I should."

"Don't be so tough on yourself. You can't be looking everywhere at once," O'Lunny said.

Onstage the murmur of voices grew louder and angrier. O'Lunny glanced over his shoulder and groaned.

"Uh-oh—Charles is on the warpath again," he said. "Come on, Frank. We'd better see if I can smooth his ruffled feathers."

As Frank and O'Lunny joined the crowd in the middle of the stage, Battenberg announced, "That dummy was meant to represent me. The assault on it was the same as an assault on *me*."

One of the chorus members near Frank muttered, "Don't we wish."

"Now, now, Charles," Hornby said. "It was just somebody's idea of a joke, that's all."

"It was a deliberate menace," Battenberg retorted. He reached down and grabbed the strand of monofilament. "And look at this. Nylon fishing line. I can't say I'm surprised. We all know which member of the cast is an ardent fisherman, don't we?"

Everyone turned to look at Ewan Gordean.

Gordean's cheeks turned dark red. "Preposterous," he snorted. He sounded more than ever like Frank's idea of Dr. Watson. "Utter nonsense! Really, Charles, you've gone too far this time."

Battenberg raised one eyebrow. "Indeed?" he said. "Do you deny that you are so besotted with fishing that you keep your rod and tackle in your dressing room? Are you trying to tell us that you never use nylon line of this sort?"

"Certainly I keep my fishing gear near at hand," Gordean said cooly. "That way, I can relax any time I get a break from working with *you*. And every fisherman I know uses monofilament leader. I bought a new spool of it only a few days ago."

"So, you admit it!" Battenberg trumpeted.

Gordean gave him a look of disdain. He said, "Think back a few minutes, Charles . . . *if* your faculties can handle anything that complicated. When that dummy fell, we were both on the other side of the stage. I was standing right next to you. Whoever made it fall, it certainly wasn't me . . . and you're my best witness to that."

Battenberg raised his right hand, with his forefinger pointing toward the ceiling. "Aha!" he exclaimed, glaring at Gordean. "That proves it! You contrived to be next to me, while one of your minions did the dirty work. Just as I thought— there's a conspiracy afoot! But I'll see to it that you don't succeed."

Someone near Frank said in a stage whisper, "Uh-oh—the Woodchuck's on the warpath again."

A burst of laughter was quickly suppressed. Frank worked out the wordplay. "Chuck" was a nickname for Charles, and "Wood" was a comment on his acting. Clever, Frank thought, as he stole a glance over his shoulder and saw that Will Robertson had made the joke. Gordean's friend and Battenberg's understudy . . . and one of the Hardys' main suspects for the role of saboteur.

O'Lunny went up to Battenberg, put his hand on his shoulder, and spoke quietly in his ear. Then he did the same to Gordean. After a pause, the two stars of the show walked off the stage— in opposite directions.

"All right, we're going on with the rehearsal," Hornby announced. "Susanna, we'll come back to your scene in a little while. Why don't we run through the scene in the warehouse when Will and Jonathan have their fight?"

Bettina walked into the middle of the crowd. Raising her voice, she said, "Clear the stage, please. All except openers for Act Three, Scene Two."

Frank and Joe left the stage right behind Hector and Susanna. Frank saw a chance to find out more about Hector. The actor had the programming skills to mess up the ticket program. But what about motive? Did he have any reason to want the play to fail?

With Joe right behind him, Frank picked up his pace and drew level with the two young actors.

"Hi," Frank said. "It's never dull around here, is it?"

Susanna made a wry face. "After the last fifteen minutes, I could use a little dullness," she said. "I really thought Charles was committing suicide, right there in front of me."

The four went into the green room. Three other Irregulars were sprawled on chairs with cans of soda in their hands. They looked up and waved to the new arrivals.

"These so-called accidents," Joe remarked, trying to strike up a conversation with the cast. "It's starting to look like somebody has it in for Battenberg."

"Or for the whole show," Frank added. "I don't know how you guys can keep your morale up, with all that's been happening."

From beside the coffee urn, Hector said, "It's not easy. But what keeps us going is that we know we've got a great show and a great cast. All we need to become a gigantic hit is a few little breaks. And we're going to get the breaks we need. Just wait and see."

"I hope so," Frank said sincerely, wondering what Hector meant about the breaks. Was he part of the conspiracy? Frank sat down on the couch next to Susanna.

Joe dragged a folding chair over near them and sat down. "I'm no expert, but I think you've got a really terrific Holmes," he said.

The statement was met with tense silence. "Charles is a good actor," Hector finally said, in a neutral voice.

"Oh, come on," one of the Irregulars said. "You know Will would be a lot better in the part. You said so yourself, just a couple of days ago."

Hector's cheeks darkened. "That was before last night, Max. You have to admit, Charles performs better in front of an audience than in rehearsal."

"But is his performance worth a million?" another Irregular asked skeptically.

Joe's eyes widened. "A million dollars? Battenberg isn't being paid that kind of money, is he?"

Susanna laughed. "No, of course not. This is the theater, not the movies. Max is just talking about a silly rumor. According to Mila, who works in the office, the production company bought a key person insurance policy on Charles. Supposedly the policy pays a million dollars if anything happens to him. Me, I don't believe it. I think it was either a publicity stunt or a ploy to make him feel more important."

"Which is about as necessary as making a London fog feel foggier," Hector said, with a wry smile.

"The next scene has fog," Joe told Frank. "From a machine."

"Sounds like fun," Frank said. He turned to Susanna and asked, "What's with Battenberg and Gordean? Why are they always at each other?"

After another tense silence, Susanna said, "Ancient history. The story I heard is that Ewan thinks Charles deliberately sabotaged a production that was supposed to be Ewan's big chance at being a star."

"Don't forget Will Robertson," Hector said. "Ewan and Will are old friends. And Will actually played Holmes in a TV movie a few years ago. He was good, too. Ewan couldn't believe it when the role went to Charles instead."

64

Susanna gave Joe and Frank a smile. "If you want to catch up on old gossip, just hang out in a theater greenroom," she said. "Not that we're all born busybodies. It's just that we have to spend so much time hanging around, waiting for our next scene. And face it, talking about other people's quirks is a lot more interesting than knitting."

A crackle of static came from a loudspeaker on the wall. Bettina's voice said, "Irregulars, get ready. Act Two, Scene Three. You're on in three minutes."

Joe jumped up from his chair.

Hector said, "Relax, Joe. Scene changes always take longer than they say." He finished his coffee, tossed the cup in the trash bin, and strolled toward the door. Joe and the other Irregulars followed him out.

"I think I'll watch," Frank told Susanna. "What about you?"

Susanna shook her head. "I need to do a little mental preparation for my next scene. I guess that falling dummy shook me more than I knew. I'll see you later."

Frank returned to a spot in the wings where he could see the stage. The scene was a back alley. Hector, Joe, and the others were in the opposite wings, ready to make their entrance.

Frank glanced around. Gordean and Robertson

were a few feet away, near the fog machine. The two actors were huddled together, talking in low voices. Gordean noticed Frank's glance and muttered something to Will. He then looked over his shoulder at Frank before turning and walking away. After a moment, Gordean followed.

Frank shrugged. Were the two actors involved in something underhanded? It certainly appeared so. The way they were behaving was almost like renting a billboard and advertising the fact.

A stagehand came by, carrying a gallon jug of water. He walked over to the fog machine, unscrewed the cap of the water tank, and started to fill it. After a few seconds, he stopped. With a surprised look on his face, he peered down into the tank. Then he replaced the cap and walked away.

The stage lights dimmed for the start of the scene. With a click, the fog generator went into action. The horn-shaped nozzle started spewing a thick gray mist onto the stage. Some of the vapor drifted over to where Frank was standing.

Frank took a breath. A sharp smell stung his nose, then his throat felt as if it were on fire. He clapped his hands over his face. A moment later, he doubled over, coughing helplessly.

7 The Fog Thickens

Coughing and blinded by tears, Frank staggered over to the fog machine. There had to be a switch on it, but where? Everything was a blur. He covered his nose and mouth with his left hand. Kneeling next to the machine, he ran his right hand over the top and sides of it. There was no switch that he could feel, but his fingertips touched the power cord. He jerked it. The machine gave a little shake and fell silent.

With the machine off, Frank could hear the coughs of the people onstage. From her command post in the opposite wing, Bettina shouted, "Clear the stage! Everybody out! Aston, Pat, get over to the loading dock and open the sliding doors. We've got to ventilate this place now!"

A group of actors hurried past Frank with tears streaming down their cheeks. From the rear of the backstage area came a rattling noise. Frank guessed that it was the loading-dock doors sliding open. A moment later he felt a breeze on his cheek. The noxious fog started to thin out.

As Frank was getting to his feet, he spotted a plastic bottle a few feet away in a dusty corner. It was lying on its side, half hidden by the folds of a curtain. It looked as though someone had hastily tossed it there.

Frank went over and picked up the bottle. The cap was off, and it was empty. The label read Spirits of Ammonia. Frank nodded to himself. He had been almost sure that he'd recognized that smell. For the sake of thoroughness, he held the mouth of the bottle a little way from his nose and took a cautious sniff.

His eyes instantly started to tear again. That was the stuff, all right. He wiped his eyes on his shirt sleeve.

Suddenly somebody tackled Frank around the waist. The sneak attack threw him backward. Frank's left shoulder crashed against the wall, and the ammonia bottle flew out of his hand.

His attacker pulled back and tried to slam him into the wall a second time. Ignoring the pain in his shoulder, Frank whacked the man on the side of the neck with the point of his elbow. There was a loud grunt, and the pressure around Frank's waist let up.

Frank was getting set to follow up with a knee to the stomach, when someone shouted, "What are you doing? Stop it at once, do you hear me?"

Frank looked around. Hornby was standing with his hands on his hips and a look of fury on his face.

The assailant released his grip and backed away. Frank was surprised to see that it was Max, one of the Irregulars who had been in the green-room a few minutes before.

"You'd better have a good explanation, Max," Hornby said coldly. "This is a theater, not a boxing arena."

Max pointed to Frank. "This piece of garbage was trying to wreck our play," he declared. "I caught him redhanded."

Hornby shifted his glare to Frank. "You're Donald's new assistant, aren't you? What do you have to say for yourself?"

"I don't know what Max's problem is," Frank said. "When I smelled the fumes, I made it over here and unplugged the fog generator before it got any worse. Then I saw an empty bottle on the floor. It smelled like ammonia. I was looking at it when Max sneaked up and grabbed me."

"He had the bottle in his hand," Max said. "And he was standing right by the fog machine.

What was I supposed to think? I still say he's the one who tried to gas us."

Hornby looked from Max to Frank and back. "Where is this mysterious bottle?" he asked.

Frank glanced around. The bottle had landed several feet away, under a table. He retrieved it. As he did, he spotted a price tag stuck to the bottom. It was from Value Plus, a chain of discount stores. One of their stores was just a few blocks from the theater, on Broad Street.

Hornby took the bottle from Frank and looked at it with a sour face.

At that moment Joe hurried over. O'Lunny was close behind him, with Bettina and the stagehand whom Frank had seen tending the fog machine earlier.

"Frank, are you okay?" Joe demanded. "What happened?"

Frank explained once more, and pointed to the bottle in Hornby's hand. "My hunch," he concluded, "is that someone poured the ammonia into the water tank of the fog generator. Then, as soon as the machine was turned on, the fumes spread across the stage."

"Someone? You mean *you*," Max said sullenly, glaring at Frank.

The others ignored him. Joe asked, "When was the machine used last?"

"During last night's performance, I imagine," O'Lunny told him.

"This morning," Bettina said. "The lighting designer turned it on so he could check one of his effects."

"And no ammonia?" O'Lunny asked.

"Nope. Just fog," Bettina replied. She glanced at the stagehand. "Right, Al?"

"Right," Al replied. "But I just thought of something. About a half hour ago, I checked the reservoir on the machine. It was half full. I meant to fill it, but then I got caught up in a couple of other jobs. When I finally got around to it, the tank was nearly full. I was kind of surprised, but I figured someone else on the crew had taken care of it."

"So it sounds as though the ammonia was probably put in the tank between the time you checked it and the time you came back to fill it," Joe said. "A little less than half an hour."

Rolling his eyes, Hornby said, "That's the trouble with doing a show about Sherlock Holmes. Everybody wants to play detective."

Frank caught Joe's eye and gave a tiny shake of the head. It was important not to do or say anything that might tip people off to their real mission.

"Come now, Gilbert," O'Lunny said. "Joe's

making a good point. If we knew where everyone was during that half hour, we would at least know who *couldn't* have pulled this stunt."

"Huh!" Hornby snorted. "We were all over the place. I must have walked past this fog machine half a dozen times. And I'll bet every one of you did, too. Enough of this. We have a rehearsal to finish."

He turned to Bettina. "Spread the word. Five more minutes, then we carry on from where we left off. *Without* the fog this time, please. And get someone to clean out the fog machine. We'll need it in working order for tonight's performance."

Bettina told Al to take the fog machine back to the scenery shop. Then she went off to carry out Hornby's orders.

Hornby glanced at the Hardys, then said to O'Lunny, "A word with you, Donald?" They walked away together.

That left Frank and Joe with Max. After giving Frank a dirty look, Max headed in the direction of the dressing rooms.

"Another hot prospect for our fan club," Joe remarked. "And speaking about hot prospects, what does this latest stunt do for our suspect list?"

Frank told him about seeing Gordean and

72

Robertson standing near the fog machine earlier. "I didn't notice either of them fiddle with it," he admitted. "But they sure didn't like it when they noticed me watching them."

"Say they're in it together," Joe said. "One of them could have acted as a combination screen and lookout while the other put the ammonia in the tank."

Frank said, "Let's try something. Stand next to the machine, with your back to the stage."

"Okay." Joe took up his position.

Frank walked out onto the stage and looked back. Then he returned to the wings and followed a semicircular path around the fog machine. Finally he rejoined Joe.

"I thought so," he said. "I couldn't see the machine from the stage, because you're in the way. And from better than half of the backstage area, you *and* the machine are hidden by that side curtain. Our trickster wasn't taking such a big risk after all."

"What about that guy who jumped you?" Joe asked. "Do you think he's part of it?"

Frank gave a short laugh. "Max? I doubt it. He's read a few too many superhero comics, that's all. When he spotted me next to the fog machine with a bottle in my hand, he saw his chance to strike a blow for Truth, Justice, and the

American Way." Frank massaged his side and added, "If only he'd struck it with a little less enthusiasm."

"Hey, I just thought of something," Joe said. "Unless he's working with somebody else, we can cross Hector off our suspect list. He's got an alibi."

"How so?" asked Frank.

Joe said, "Think back. After the fight between Battenberg and Gordean, we went back to the greenroom with Hector. He didn't leave the room while we were there. I went out onstage with him to rehearse our scene, and that's where we were when the fog started. So there wasn't any time when he could have come over here to doctor the fog machine."

Frank frowned thoughtfully. "That's right," he said. "Or nearly right. Why couldn't he have put in the ammonia while the rest of us were onstage, listening to the argument? Who would have noticed?"

"Um," Joe said. "Yeah, okay . . . but that would mean having the stuff someplace nearby and moving awfully fast. Even if we don't cross him off the list completely, I still think this moves him down a few places, especially since we don't have any motive for him at this point."

"We don't have a strong motive for anyone,"

Frank pointed out. "Except general dislike for Battenberg."

"Joe?" Hector called, from the edge of the stage. "Come on. We're starting."

Joe jumped. "Oh, okay—thanks," he called back. To Frank, he said, "I've got to go. What are you going to do?"

"I think I'll pay a visit to Ewan Gordean's dressing room," Frank replied. "If he's there, I'll ask him a few questions. And if he isn't . . . well, it wouldn't hurt to take a look around."

Joe joined the other Irregulars onstage. Frank watched them do their number for a few moments. Then he walked down the hallway that led to the dressing rooms. Each of the doors had a little brass holder for a name tag. Gordean's held an engraved calling card.

Frank rapped on the door and listened, hearing only silence inside. He looked both ways, then tried the knob. It gave a loud squeal and turned. He pushed the door open a crack. The room was dark.

Frank said, "Hello?" No answer. He slipped inside and shut the door behind him. Then he groped along the wall for the light switch, found it, and flicked it on.

"*Whoa!*" Frank gasped. As the ceiling light came on, the first thing he saw was the looming

75

form of someone only a few feet from him. An instant later he realized that he was looking at his own distorted image in a mirror that covered an entire wall. He took a deep breath and waited for his pulse to calm down. Then he looked around.

The room was small, no more than six feet wide by nine feet long. The floor was bare concrete, and the pale green walls and ceiling looked as if they had last been painted seventy-five years ago, when the Orpheum was still showing vaudeville. The mirror was on the long wall, to the right of the door. Just below the mirror, at sitting height, was a long shelf littered with bottles and tubes of makeup. At the far end of the room, a sheet suspended from the ceiling partly hid some costumes on hangers.

A brown metal folding chair was drawn up in front of the makeup table. The only other piece of furniture was a sagging armchair covered in faded floral chintz. A little stack of paperback mysteries sat on the floor next to it.

In the corner behind the door, Frank spotted the canvas case of a fishing rod and a gray metal tackle box. So Gordean really did keep his fishing gear handy. Frank went over, bent down, and lifted the lid of the tackle box.

The top shelf in the box contained a neatly arranged assortment of lures. Frank lifted it out. The main compartment, underneath, was more disordered. There was an expensive spinning reel, a rusty folding knife, a tiny can of lubricating oil, an oil-stained rag, and a bunch of other stuff. Everything had a faintly fishy smell. Frank sifted through it. Near the bottom, he spotted a dark blue plastic spool. He lifted it out. The label read Monofilament Leader, 50-lb. Test. The spool was almost empty. Another spool near it looked unused.

Frank replaced the two spools and sat back on his heels to think. Was the empty one the source of the nylon line used to rig the dummy? And if so, did that mean that Gordean was responsible? Or did it even, in a way, show that he was innocent? Would anyone who was guilty keep such obvious evidence around where anyone could find it?

Footsteps stopped outside the door, and Frank was all ears.

He heard the doorknob squeal and took in a quick breath.

Someone was coming into the room.

8 Moriarty's Curse

The dressing-room door started to swing open. Frank was trapped, caught redhanded . . . or was he? He could see one slim chance to escape exposure—his only chance.

Frank jumped to his feet and made a silent dash the length of the room. Ducking behind the sheet that formed the front of the improvised closet, he quickly burrowed to the back of the row of costumes. They were dusty and smelled of greasepaint. He stood still and tried to breathe silently through his mouth.

Oh, no! he thought. The tackle box! He hadn't had time to close the lid. Gordean would notice it immediately. He would know someone had been in his dressing room. Would he search the room himself, or call for help?

Frank heard Gordean say, "You can't hide that way forever, you know."

Frank's pulse raced. He hadn't expected Gordean to spot him *that* quickly. Were his shoes showing under the row of costumes?

He was about to step out from behind the curtain when he heard the murmur of a second voice. With a rush of relief, Frank realized that Gordean had been talking to someone else. He *hadn't* discovered Frank—not yet at least.

Gordean said, "People do notice your reactions, even if you try to conceal them."

Another murmur.

"Tershous?" Gordean said. "I'd be very careful if I were you. An impressive talent, no doubt of that, but erratic. Not, in my view, to be trusted."

Frank strained his ears to hear the other half of the conversation, but all he picked up was more murmuring. He couldn't even be sure whether Gordean was talking to a man or a woman.

Gordean lowered his voice. "You know how much this role means to me. But I'm becoming more and more sure of one thing. The only chance this show has to survive is if some anonymous benefactor does a Moriarty on the Prince of Wales. And I don't know that we dare hope for that."

The door closed. Frank held his breath and waited for Gordean to notice the open tackle box. Instead, Gordean muttered, "Oh, bother!" A moment later, the door opened and shut again.

Frank risked peeking out between two of the tweed suits. The dressing room was empty. Obviously Gordean had forgotten something and had left to get it. How long would it take him? Five minutes? One? Less?

Slipping out of his hiding place, Frank hurried on tiptoes toward the door. He paused to close the lid of the tackle box. As he did, he noticed a crumpled plastic shopping bag in the wastebasket. He grabbed it and shoved it in his pocket. Then he cautiously pulled the door open a crack and peered down the hall both ways. The corridor was empty. He slipped out and pulled the door closed behind him. Turning right, he walked in the direction of the stage.

Frank hadn't taken more than two or three steps when he saw Gordean coming toward him. The actor had a script in his hand and a look of preoccupation on his face. He paid no attention to Frank at all.

Frank kept walking, as casually as possible. As soon as he heard Gordean's dressing-room door close, he took a deep breath and let it out slowly. That had been a little too close.

What had Gordean meant by his last remark? Frank wondered. The part about Moriarty wasn't hard to figure out. Professor Moriarty was the criminal mastermind who had tried to murder Sherlock Holmes by pushing him over the edge of a waterfall. But what did the Prince of Wales have to do with it?

"Ha!" Frank said, as the answer came to him. The Prince of Wales, of course, was Prince Charles. And Frank remembered that the family name of Prince Charles's father was Mountbatten or, in the original German, Battenberg. So the Prince of Wales was a perfect nickname for Charles Battenberg!

That left a couple of big questions. When Gordean wished for a Moriarty, did he really mean that he wanted someone to kill Battenberg? If so, was he simply wishing, or was he secretly trying to make his wish come true? And how was the person named Tershous connected?

As Frank drew closer to the stage, he saw Susanna standing in the wings, watching the rehearsal. She noticed him and smiled. "Hi," she said in a low voice, when he joined her. "How's it going?"

Frank replied, "I was about to ask you that."

"No more dummies, gas attacks, or falling scenery," Susanna told him. "So far. I guess we should be grateful for small favors. It's funny—I always dreamed of working in theater. I never thought that it would be like this."

"It'll all get straightened out," Frank said.

Susanna shook her head. "Don't I wish! Still, it could be worse. Imagine how poor Hector feels."

"Why?" Frank asked.

"You didn't know?" Susanna replied. "He turned down a juicy supporting role in a TV series to take this part. It was just the pilot, but if it went over, he'd be set for years. And what does he have instead? Third billing in a musical that'll probably close in out-of-town tryouts. Not a great swap."

"Could he still change his mind?" Frank asked.

"Take the TV role, you mean?" Susanna said. "I don't know. It might still be open, I guess. But it wouldn't matter. He can't walk out on his contract here. If he did that, he'd be finished in show business."

Frank was thinking that there was an obvious solution to Hector's problem. But he kept it to himself. There wasn't much Hector could do to make *The Giant Rat of Sumatra* a hit . . . but he could do any number of things to make it a failure. And that failure could mean success for him!

When the rehearsal ended, Hornby and O'Lunny gave the cast a pep talk, then sent everyone off to rest for the evening performance.

Joe and Frank wanted to hang around and contin-
ue their investigation. But O'Lunny took them
aside and said that it would look more natural if
they left, too.

During the drive home, Frank gave Joe a full
report on his visit to Gordean's dressing room. As
a finale, he pulled the wadded up shopping bag
from his pocket and said, "And look, Joe. I found
this in Gordean's wastebasket. It's from Value
Plus. That's where that ammonia came from."

Joe glanced over, then returned his eyes to the
road. "The shopping bag, the empty spool of
leader," he said. "Gordean's dressing room was
full of evidence against him. Are you sure he
didn't write on the mirror, 'Stop me before I
commit more acts of sabotage'?"

Frank laughed and said, "You think it sounds
like a frame, don't you?"

Joe thought for a moment before saying, "Well,
yes, I guess I do. I mean, everybody knows
Gordean's heavy into fishing. Why would he go
out of his way to use that leader, knowing it would
point straight to him? And the ammonia—why
leave the bottle where it was bound to be spotted,
with the price tag still on it, and then toss the bag
in your own dressing-room wastebasket?"

"Crooks do sometimes make stupid mistakes,"
Frank pointed out.

Joe said, "Sure—starting with the decision to

turn crooked in the first place. But the guy we're after is obviously pretty smart, if he's avoided getting caught for this long. But the business with the fishing leader is just a little too dumb. It smells of frame."

"Well, maybe you're right," Frank conceded. "But I still think there's something there. When we get home, we should try to find out who Tershous is. That's the person Gordean told his friend not to trust. I don't know where that piece fits in this puzzle, but I'm willing to bet that it fits somewhere."

Once home, Joe and Frank said hi to their mother, snagged a couple of pieces of their aunt Gertrude's cherry pie and a half-gallon of milk from the fridge, and headed for their basement crime lab. Joe booted the computer and ate some pie while he waited. He took a drink of milk, then logged onto the World Wide Web. Ninety seconds later he was studying the home page of America's leading theatrical newspaper.

"What was that name again?" he asked, as he clicked on the Index.

"It sounded like Tershous," Frank replied. "I've never heard of it before, though."

Joe scanned the *T* entries in the index. "Neither has this paper," he reported. "I'll try using the search engine."

He typed in the name and pressed Return. Almost instantly, the search turned up a near-hit.

"Lestell, Tertius," he read aloud. "Producer-director. There's a hyperlink to his home page."

Joe clicked on the link to Lestell's page, with Frank looking over his shoulder. What came up on the screen was a brief biography, a list of plays Lestell had produced or directed, and a photo that showed a tall bald man with a wide smile, surrounded by a dozen admirers.

"Frank, look," Joe said, pointing to one of the people in the photo, a short stout man standing next to Tertius. "Isn't that Ewan Gordean?"

"At this resolution, I couldn't swear to it," Frank replied. "It does look like him, though. But if he's such a buddy of this guy Lestell, why was he warning somebody against him?"

"That's for him to know and us to find out," Joe said. "And we'd better start to work on it the minute we get back to the Orpheum."

After an early dinner, Joe and Frank drove back to the theater. As they signed in, the stage-door guard said, "You fellows are among the first to come in. I was starting to wonder if they'd called off tonight's show and forgotten to tell me."

"Do you know if Mr. O'Lunny is here yet?" Frank asked.

The guard laughed. "You bet—he practically lives here! You'll probably find him in the office. You know where that is?"

"Sure, thanks," Frank said. As he and Joe walked down the hall, Frank said, "I thought I'd try to get the story on Lestell. You want to tag along or do some scouting around?"

"I'll scout and then get back to you," Joe said.

Joe wandered through the backstage area, watching for anything out of the ordinary. He was still surprised by how big the rear area of the theater was. From the audience, the stage looked small, but it actually took up just as much space as the auditorium itself.

Joe approached the corridor that led to the dressing rooms. At the far end of the hall, someone was bending down next to one of the doors. Joe stepped back out of sight, then peered around the corner. He was just in time to see the person hurry away. The light was too dim for him to identify more than a vague form.

Joe walked down the hall to the door. From under it, the corner of an envelope stuck out. He looked both ways, then knelt down and fished it out. The flap wasn't stuck down, but rather tucked inside. Joe opened it and found a typed note inside. It read, "The evidence you need is inside the pub."

He glanced at the cardholder on the door. It confirmed it was Battenberg's dressing room, which didn't surprise Joe. Apparently some friend who wanted to stay anonymous had decided to help Battenberg solve the mystery.

"Inside the pub," Joe read again, recalling that the street scene in the second act included a pub. But the actors never actually went inside it. He wasn't even sure that what looked like the door to the pub really opened.

Only one way to find out. He put the envelope back where he had found it. Then he returned to the stage. It was set up again as Holmes's sitting room. The street scene was in back, on the turntable. In the half darkness, Joe walked over to the pub and tried the door. It resisted for a moment, then swung open.

Joe stepped inside and looked warily around. He was in a narrow space between two sets of tall wood and canvas flats. The closest thing he saw to evidence was a couple of crumpled candy wrappers on the floor and a footprint in the dust. Was that worth a closer look? He walked toward it.

Joe's stomach lurched as the floor gave way under his foot. Dimly, in the back of his mind, he realized someone had rigged a false floor. He was falling through painted canvas over an open trapdoor!

9 Left Hanging

Joe thrust his arms out to either side in an effort to stop his fall. How wide was the hole in the floor? His life might depend on the answer to that question.

He felt the shock as his elbows and forearms smashed against the floorboards. Pain raced through his upper arms and shoulders, then down the long muscles of his back. All his weight was suspended from his outstretched arms. It was like doing a chin up with some overweight pizza lover clinging to your ankles.

"Help!" Joe shouted. He took a deep breath and shouted again. "Somebody, *help!*"

There was no response. Joe knew his calls for help were muffled by the sets that loomed over him. He would have to get out of his dire situation on his own.

Did he dare let himself drop? Joe's martial arts training had taught him how to fall and do a tuck and roll. If he were faced with jumping from a second-floor window to the ground, he would have simply counted to three and jumped. But to jump from an unknown height, to an unknown surface, that was another matter. At best he could expect to land on concrete and shatter a few bones. And what if the dark space below him was filled with sharp-angled machinery?

His arms felt as if they were being slowly pulled out of his shoulder sockets. He couldn't keep up the downward pressure for much longer. It would be so easy to relax, to let his arms fold up over his head and to slide through the hole in the floor to . . .

No! Joe clenched his teeth and tried to push himself up. The veins in his neck felt ready to explode. After three seconds he knew that it wasn't going to work. He didn't have the leverage it would take to lift his weight up out of the hole.

If he couldn't lift himself, could he somehow manage to throw himself? He remembered watching an Olympic pole-vaulting competition on TV. In his mind he saw the athletes twist themselves upward, almost vertically, and fling first their feet, then their curved bodies, over the horizontal barrier. Could he manage to do something like that?

Slowly, carefully, he set his body swinging forward and backward. The motion put an intense new strain on his arms and shoulders, and he knew he couldn't keep it up for long. He would have one shot at making his goal, no more.

He waited until his legs were at the very peak of their swing backward. As his body, like a pendulum, began to swing down and forward, he pulled his knees up and jackknifed at the waist. Joe threw his head backward to give added leverage to the movement.

Now! Joe straightened his legs at the knees and swung them up with all his strength. It worked. His legs had cleared the edge of the opening. Gratefully he felt the solid floor under his heels and calves. But he wasn't out of danger yet. Most of his body was still hanging in space, supported by his failing arms.

Joe grabbed a deep breath and arched his back. Pushing off with his right arm, he rolled to the left. For one awful moment he felt himself start to fall again. He made one last frantic twist. Then he lay stretched out on his side, panting.

How long was it before he felt he could try to stand up? A minute? Two or three? He never knew. And when he did push himself to his feet, wincing at the ache in his shoulders, he had to stand still until the ground stopped spinning.

Carefully skirting the open pit in the floor, he pulled open the pub door and stepped out onto the stage just as Bettina, the stage manager, came in his direction.

"Hey, what were you doing back there?" Bettina asked, giving him a suspicious look.

"Nearly getting myself killed," Joe responded. "Look—that trapdoor's open."

Bettina looked. "Uh-oh," she said. "I'd better take care of that. I wonder how it happened—not that it would have mattered if people kept out of places where they're not supposed to be."

She walked quickly toward the raised platform that served her as a control booth. Joe kept pace with her. "How do those trapdoors work?" he asked.

She glanced over at him. "Each one has a motor to open and shut it," she told him. "They're controlled from a panel at my desk. Down in the basement there's a movable scaffold with a platform that rises. It's all pretty primitive. This house hasn't been used for theatrical productions in thirty years or more."

"So there was a platform under me the whole time?" Joe asked. He was slightly disappointed that the danger he'd escaped wasn't more spectacular.

"I didn't say that," Bettina said. "We're not using the scaffold, so it's pushed over to the side, out of the way. If you'd gone through the trap, you would have fallen twenty feet to a cement floor."

Joe gulped. "Oh," he said. Somehow that didn't make him feel any better. "Well, thanks. I'll see you." He crossed the stage and headed for the hallway that led to the dressing rooms. His first job was to retrieve the envelope from under Battenberg's door—if it was still there. Someone had quite possibly lured him to the trapdoor. Whether the person wanted Joe or Battenberg to take the plunge wasn't clear. Why hadn't he tried to get a closer look at the person who'd left it there? Joe felt frustrated. He couldn't even be sure whether it had been a man or a woman.

The corner of the envelope was still sticking out from under the door. Joe fished it out and continued down the hall to the office. Inside, Frank and O'Lunny were talking. When Joe walked in, O'Lunny looked up and said, "Joe—is anything wrong?"

Joe told them about his adventure and showed them the note.

Frank studied it for a moment, then turned and typed the contents on the office computer. After printing it, he looked at the output and said, "Identical. Here, see for yourselves."

Joe took the note, put the new printout on top of it, and held the two pages up against the light. "You're right," he said.

"Most laser printers have a Times Roman font built in," O'Lunny said. "I know the one I have at home does."

"True, but the same font can be a little different from one printer to another," Frank told him. "These printouts aren't absolute proof. But it looks as if whoever wanted to make Battenberg or Joe fall through that open trapdoor also had access to this office."

O'Lunny looked gloomy. "That eliminates all but about two dozen people," he said. "Namely, the entire cast and crew of *The Giant Rat of Sumatra.* We lock the door when we know no one will be around, sure. But during run-throughs and performances, it's usually open. People feel free to wander in and out. They don't even—"

Just then the door flew open and banged against the wall. Li Wei rushed in. She stared at O'Lunny with narrowed eyes and said, "Do you realize what that idiot Hornby is planning to do?"

"Oh, hello, Li," O'Lunny said. "Have you met Joe and Frank Hardy? They've just joined us."

Li Wei continued to stare at O'Lunny. "So you do know," she said tautly. "In other words, you agree."

"You mean, about cutting 'Foggy River'?" O'Lunny replied. "No, frankly, I don't. It's one of our best songs—"

"*The* best," Li Wei interrupted.

O'Lunny raised his hands, palms upward. "Could be," he said. "I told Gilbert how good it was when he suggested cutting it. I could tell he liked it, too. But it doesn't matter. Our star has taken a violent dislike to the song. He flatly refuses to sing it. What was Gilbert to do?"

"Fire Battenberg for breach of contract," Li Wei retorted.

"Just when we have a chance at Broadway?" O'Lunny said. "Please, be serious. But I promise you this, Li. If for any reason Charles leaves the cast, 'Foggy River' will go back into the play."

Li Wei stood tense and silent for a long moment. She seemed to be collecting herself. Then she looked at O'Lunny and said, "Poor Donald. You don't realize it yet, but you'd be so much better off if something or somebody made Hornby drop out from the play. The rights would revert to you, and you'd find a new and better producer within twenty-four hours. Why are you so loyal to a fool like Hornby?"

"I value loyalty," O'Lunny said simply. "And

if I'm loyal to my teammates, they're more likely to be loyal to me. Don't you agree?"

Li Wei gave him a long cold look. Then she whirled around and stalked out of the office.

O'Lunny stared blankly at the empty doorway. Then he shook his head and looked over at Joe and Frank. "I'm sorry, fellows," he said. "I need a few minutes to think."

"Of course," Frank said. "Just one question. Does the name Lestell ring a bell with you?"

O'Lunny blinked. "Tertius Lestell? Of course. He's a well-known producer. He and Gilbert used to be partners, as a matter of fact. Then they had a falling out. I don't know the details. I do know what everyone in show business knows: they hate each other. Either of them would do anything to see the other one fall on his face."

As curtain time drew near, Frank prowled around, on the watch for anything that seemed out of the ordinary. Joe was back in the dressing room, getting into his costume and makeup. The mood backstage was excited. A little *too* excited?

Frank wasn't sure. Maybe the frantic feeling was normal for one of the first performances of a new play. Still, there was a hectic note in the way the cast members spoke, a certain jerkiness in the way they moved, that seemed almost feverish. They were like the audience at a horror flick, both expecting and dreading that something terrible was about to happen.

"Openers, places, please," a crew member announced.

Battenberg and Gordean walked out onstage into Holmes's living room and sat down at a small round dining table. Gordean picked up a copy of the London *Times,* and Battenberg filled a pipe with tobacco.

A table with all the props on it was a few feet behind Frank. Celia Hatteras stopped at it and picked up a tray loaded with cups, saucers, plates, and a teapot. She looked it over. Frowning, she said, "Props? I'm missing a teaspoon."

One of the crew hurried to her side. "I checked it just ten minutes ago," he said.

"There's only one spoon," Ms. Hatteras pointed out. "Mrs. Hudson needs two—one for each of them."

"I'll get another in half a mo'," the stagehand said. He rushed off.

Frank could hear the murmur of the audience through the curtain. It seemed to be getting stronger and more impatient. Frank noticed that all of a sudden the lights aimed at Holmes's breakfast table grew brighter. Then he heard a loud crackle and saw a blue flash.

The stage was plunged into darkness.

10 Crossed Circuits

A babble of confused and alarmed voices rose from the theater. Dim emergency lights came on, and someone went out through the curtain to apologize to the audience. The uproar gradually subsided.

Frank dashed across the stage toward the light booth. Bettina was just ahead of him. "What happened?" he asked when he caught up to her.

"When I find out myself, I'll tell you," she answered. She sounded angry. "I *knew* we were going to have trouble with that light board. It's so old, it was probably installed by Thomas Edison himself!"

The light booth was a platform three steps up from the stage, with a railing of two-by-fours around it. The control board was a confusing array of switches and dials, each labeled with a ragged strip of masking tape.

Frank followed Bettina up into the booth. The man who stood behind it was about twenty-five. He had silver rings in his left ear and was wearing black jeans, a black T-shirt with the logo of a heavy metal group, and black parachute boots. He looked a little dazed.

"Okay, Jeff, what's the story?" Bettina asked.

He looked around at her and blinked a few times. "Beats me," he said. "I started bringing up the number-three pot for the curtain, and *bam!* All the circuit breakers blew."

Frank knew that *pot* was an abbreviated form of the word *potentiometer*. The pots were manipulated to control the lights.

"Okay, Jeff, we have about ninety seconds to find and fix the problem," Bettina said tersely. "You got a flash?"

Jeff reached under the light board and produced a big four-cell krypton flashlight, the kind highway patrolmen carry. Bettina grabbed it out of his hand, went to the side of the board, and shone the light on the back. Frank leaned over and craned his neck to see.

"Bettina?" he said. "Why is that metal teaspoon lying across those wires?"

Bettina said, "I guess you're not as useless as

you look. Jeff, pass me some kind of tool with an insulated handle."

Jeff handed her a rubber-handled screwdriver. She reached down and flicked the teaspoon off the wires. It clattered to the floor. Frank bent down to pick it up, then held it in the beam of the flashlight. The surface of the metal had a bluish sheen.

"You have to get stainless steel really hot for it to take on that color," Frank said.

Bettina glanced at the spoon, but she obviously had other things on her mind. She turned to Jeff and said, "Reset the circuit breakers, starting with the main. Let's find out if we're going to be able to do a show tonight."

Jeff stretched to reach the row of switches near the top of the board. He carefully flipped each one in turn.

Bettina stood watching tensely as the stage lights came on again. "Okay, we're in business," she finally said. She turned to go, saying, "Carry on."

Frank held up a hand. "Bettina, how did that spoon get there?"

She shrugged. "I guess somebody left it on the board and it fell in back. Murphy's Law: If anything can possibly go wrong, it will. Excuse me—we've got a show to put on." She hurried off.

99

Frank turned to Jeff. "Just a couple of questions," he said. "Did anyone come visit you in the booth in the last half hour or so?"

Jeff gave him a sidelong look. "Visit? Not really," he said. "One of the cast came by to ask about a lighting cue."

"Do you know his name?" Frank asked, masking his eagerness.

"Sure," Jeff replied. "He's Sherlock's understudy. Will something-or-other."

"Robertson," Frank said, nodding to himself. "And that's it? No one else?"

"That's it," Jeff told him. "Oh—and Donald O'Lunny came by to shake my hand and wish me luck. Nice guy, not stuck up at all."

Frank frowned. "Oh? Does he usually do that?"

Jeff said, "I don't know—last night he didn't, tonight he did. What about it?"

"Oh, nothing," Frank said quickly. "Who brought you the coffee?" He pointed to a paper cup on the shelf next to the light board.

"Nobody did," Jeff said. "I went to the green-room and got it for myself. Why? Oh, I get it—you're wondering if somebody put that spoon there intentionally. Well, you may be onto something. It's hard to see how the spoon could land in that particular spot, all on its own."

A green light appeared on the board.

"Sorry," Jeff added, reaching out with both hands to grasp two dimmer knobs. "That's my first cue."

The play started. As the by now familiar strains of "Kippers and Eggs" began, Frank circled behind the set to his usual station in the wings at stage left. The teaspoon was in his pocket.

O'Lunny came up beside him. "Only ten minutes late," he said in an undertone. "For a preview, that's practically on time. I dread to think what the next problem will be."

Frank glanced over at him and stiffened. O'Lunny was wearing a blue flannel blazer. Frank recalled seeing it on him before. What he didn't recall seeing were the white dots on the right sleeve. They stretched from the elbow down and thickened near the cuff. It was exactly the pattern you would expect to see if someone had worn the blazer while using a spray can of white paint to write graffiti on the set.

Frank tried to think of a way to get a sample of the white dots. What if he tugged at his collar, complained about how warm it was in the theater, and offered to hold O'Lunny's coat for him? Could he start to shiver, then ask to borrow O'Lunny's jacket for warmth?

Finally deciding the direct approach was best, Frank blurted out, "What are those white spots on the sleeve of your jacket?"

101

O'Lunny raised his arm to look, then shrugged. "I don't know," he said. "I hope they come out. This is my favorite blazer."

"Let's see." Frank grasped the sleeve in his left hand and scraped at the dots with his right forefinger. Some of them flaked off into his palm. "It should be okay."

Turning away, Frank fished a plastic bag from his pocket and dusted the flakes into it. O'Lunny was too busy watching the stage to notice.

To Frank's relief, the play went off without a single incident. The finale was as rousing as ever, and so was the applause. After the last curtain call, Joe came offstage with a big grin on his face. "Hey, I could get into this performing," he told Frank.

"Don't," Frank said. "You're enough of a ham already."

A stream of well-wishers was flowing into the backstage area. One of them, tall and bald, caught Frank's attention . . . and everyone else's. He was wearing a black cape lined with red satin over his white tie and tails, and he held a silk top hat in his left hand.

"Frank!" Joe whispered. "That's the guy in the photo—Tertius Lestell! What's he doing here?"

As Lestell was shaking hands with the actors and congratulating them, Hornby came rushing over. He was trying to look impassive, but Frank could see the vein in his temple throbbing.

"Well, Tertius," Hornby said. "Have you come to learn what real theater is from next season's biggest hit?"

Lestell gave him a smug smile and said, "This is a holiday for me. I'm spending a few days in Bayport, at the Waterside Inn, and I thought I could use some amusement. Charming place, the Waterside Inn. I recommend it."

As Lestell repeated the name of the Waterside Inn, it seemed to Frank that he looked directly at someone in the crowd. Frank tried to see whose eye he was meeting, but he couldn't.

A few minutes later Lestell left. Frank followed him outside, at a distance, and saw him get into a white stretch limousine. The license plate read LESTELL1.

Fifteen minutes later Joe pulled up at a traffic light and turned to stare at Frank. "You suspect *O'Lunny?*" he exclaimed. "But he's the one who asked us to take on the case!"

Frank said, "I don't exactly suspect him. But from what Li Wei said earlier, he has a motive. He doesn't seem to enjoy working with Hornby or Battenberg. O'Lunny had the opportunity to short the light board. And there were those spots on his jacket. What bothers me is that we didn't notice them last night when we discovered the graffiti."

The light turned green. As he started across the intersection, Joe said, "He had his raincoat on. Remember?"

"Hey, that's right," Frank said. "I wonder if Dad's friend Mr. Hiroto would be willing to put the samples through a gas chromatograph analysis for us, even though it's the weekend. We should give him a call first thing in the morning."

"Okay. But we shouldn't ignore our other suspects," Joe said. "Hector, for instance. If the play fails, he may get to do that TV role."

"There's evidence against Gordean, too," Frank pointed out. "I know you think he may have been framed, but that doesn't mean we should forget about him. What I'd like to know is who Lestell was telling to get in touch with him at the Waterside Inn just now. Gordean? O'Lunny? Hector?"

Joe smiled. "Well—we can't tap his phone. But there's nothing to stop us from hanging around the Waterside Inn tomorrow morning and seeing if he meets anybody we know."

The next morning was cloudy, but by the time Joe and Frank had driven across town to the harbor, the sun had come out. They parked the van next to the marina, across the street from the Waterside Inn, and settled down to watch the boats and wait.

The Waterside Inn was a white frame building with green shutters and a wide veranda. It had been an important town landmark since the days when Bayport's whaling ships had successfully prowled the world's oceans in search of prey.

Joe opened a Thermos and poured two cups of coffee. As he handed one to Frank, he said, "The inn's a nice place, but I can't see someone like Lestell coming here for a vacation. He probably owns his own island in the Caribbean."

"Bayport's closer," Frank said. "Look—we're just in time. There's his limo."

The long white car pulled up the drive and stopped next to the inn's front steps. Lestell must have been waiting at the entrance, because he came out the door and down the steps immediately. He got into the limo, and it purred away. Joe gave it a half-block lead, then followed.

A few minutes later he said, "He's headed for downtown. Look, we're nearly at the theater."

"And to the Madison Hotel, where most of the cast is staying," Frank added.

The limo turned onto Madison Street and pulled over to the curb. Joe stopped a few spaces back. Who would come out to meet Lestell? Gordean? His friend, Robertson? Or even Donald O'Lunny?

A moment later the Hardys had their answer. A slim woman in a scarf and dark glasses came out of the hotel and hurried over to the limo. The door opened, she ducked inside, and the powerful car sped away.

"That was Li Wei!" Joe exclaimed, as he started the van. The limo already had a two-block lead. Joe accelerated and pulled out of his space.

A second later Frank shouted, "Joe, look out!"

A big black sedan was passing them on the left. It abruptly swerved to the right, cutting Joe off. Reflexively, Joe spun the steering wheel to avoid being hit. Tires screamed as Joe slammed on the brakes. The van skidded sideways, toward the sidewalk, where a woman and a young boy were standing, frozen in shock.

Joe pumped the brakes harder as the van's right front tire rolled up onto the curb, only inches from the woman and her child.

11 A Deadly Merry-Go-Round

Frank saw the woman and boy loom closer as he sat in the passenger seat, feeling panic-stricken and helpless. Joe was wrestling grimly with the steering wheel, trying to steer the van away from the woman and child.

Finally the van came to a shuddering halt. One of the hubcaps flew off and went clattering down the street. Frank could smell scorched rubber from the tires.

Joe took a deep breath when he saw that the woman and child were out of harm's way on the sidewalk. A man rushed over to them and led them away from the scene.

"Good save," Frank said. "I thought we were going to hit that woman and kid for sure."

Joe shook his head. "That was *way* too close for comfort. I can't believe that turkey in the black sedan who cut us off. He didn't even slow down to see if we were okay. Which we almost weren't." Joe looked out Frank's window and saw that the people were gone. He wanted to apologize to them.

"I can believe it," Frank replied. "You didn't have time to see the license plate, did you? It read LESTELL2. Lestell must have noticed that somebody was tailing him and used his car phone to call in some interference."

Joe smiled grimly. "Yeah, well, we got a good look at the person who got into the limo with him. She's going to have to do some explaining. I'll go chase our hubcap," Joe added, reaching for the door latch. "You check out the tires, okay?"

Frank got out and checked all four tires, which were still sound. He gave them a couple of kicks, then returned to his seat. A few moments later Joe tossed the dented hubcap in the rear of the van and climbed behind the wheel.

"So it was Li Wei who had a date with Lestell," Joe remarked, as he started the engine. "I wasn't expecting that."

"Me, neither," Frank admitted. "On the other hand, she was seriously ticked off at Battenberg and Hornby over getting rid of her favorite song.

108

I don't know if she was mad enough to try to wreck the show, though."

"But, Frank," Joe said, "they only ditched her song yesterday, right? So why would she pull the dirty tricks that happened earlier?"

Frank thought hard. "What if she's not the only one who's in cahoots with Lestell? There's Gordean, for example. We know from the photo on Lestell's Web page that they're linked in some way. Or what about Hector?"

"Pretty soon, we're going to be suspecting everyone, even ourselves," Joe grumbled. "I've still got some time before my rehearsal. Where to?"

"Let's go home and call Mr. Hiroto," Frank suggested.

Hiroto, a forensic chemist, agreed to run the analysis of the paint flecks. The Hardys drove by his lab with the two plastic bags of specimens. When Hiroto saw how little there was, he raised his eyebrows.

"I can't promise anything," he said. "But I'll try. Where can I reach you later this afternoon?"

Frank gave him their number and added, "If we're not home, the machine will be on. And thanks for your help. We appreciate it."

"Thank your father," Hiroto replied. "I'm doing it for him."

As they drove downtown to the theater, Joe

said, "Don't get me wrong, it's a kick being in the *Rat*. But it keeps getting in the way of our investigation. If I'm not rehearsing, I'm learning my entrances or studying my lines or putting on makeup. When do I get to question suspects?"

Frank grinned. "Now, for a start. You're one of the cast. You can talk to them without anyone getting suspicious and clamming up. What do they know about Lestell? What are they worried about? What's the latest gossip? Oh, right—and do any of them have white specks on their sleeves?"

"Okay, okay," Joe said. "I'll get with the program. What about you?"

"It's a long shot, but I'm going to try to check out that bottle of ammonia," Frank told him. "I also want to do a little snooping in the office."

Joe parked the van behind the theater and they went inside. The first person they saw was Hector. He grabbed Joe's elbow and said, "A couple of things we need to talk over before the rehearsal." They went off together.

Frank watched them go. Then he walked back to the office. The door was closed, and there was no answer when he knocked. He waited a moment, then used his key to go in.

The file cabinet in the corner was not locked. He started at the bottom and checked each drawer. The file he was looking for was in the second drawer from the top. It was labeled Publicity Pix. Frank took it to the desk and started to sort through it. He took out head shots of Battenberg and Gordean, then one of Robertson.

As he was adding a photo of Li Wei to the pile, the office door swung open and in walked Hornby. When he saw Frank, he asked gruffly, "What are you doing here?"

Covering the pile with his hand, Frank said, "Mr. O'Lunny asked me to pick up some photos of the cast for him."

Hornby continued to look unhappy. "Well, in the future," he said, "remember that those files are confidential. If you need something in there, wait until someone is here to get it for you. Is that understood?"

"Yes, sir," Frank replied. "Sorry." He replaced the file, picked up the photos, and walked out. What a grouch!

After leaving the theater, Frank walked over to Broad Street. There was only one clerk inside the Value Plus store, a middle-aged man wearing a bright green jacket with the company emblem on the pocket. His face brightened when he saw Frank. "Can I help you with anything?" he asked.

"I hope so," Frank said. "Do you recall any-body buying a bottle of ammonia in the last couple of days?"

"Are you kidding?" the man retorted. "Do you have any idea how many sales we make in a day? I've got enough to do without trying to remember them all."

Frank said, "I can understand that. But would you take a look at these pictures? Do any of these people look familiar?"

The man looked through the photos twice. He shook his head. "I'm not saying they haven't been in," he told Frank. "But I sure can't say that they have. Sorry."

"That's okay. Thanks for trying," Frank said, and left the store. Out on the sidewalk, he paused in frustration. The ammonia bottle was appar-ently a dead end. What now? There were just too many unanswered questions about the links among their different suspects. But how could he get the information he needed without destroy-ing his cover?

Frank glanced down at the photos in his hand and an idea suddenly came to him. If the office kept publicity photos of the play's creators and stars on file, it probably kept press biographies of them, too—if not in the files, then on the com-puter. By examining dates and activities, he could track down people's earlier associations.

With fresh determination, he turned and walked briskly in the direction of the Orpheum Theater.

"Last night went pretty well," Joe said, "at least after they fixed the lights. Why shouldn't tonight go just as well?"

He was in the greenroom with Susanna, Hector, and several other members of the chorus. The mood was tense.

"Don't!" Susanna gasped. "Never say that a performance is going to go well. That's the second most important rule in theater."

"Oh? What's the most important?" Joe asked curiously.

"Never quote from *Macbeth*," Hector said. "That's one-hundred-percent guaranteed bad luck. And the last thing this production needs is *more* bad luck."

Jerry, one of the Irregulars, said, "What it does need is a new title. I think *The Giant Rat of Sumatra* is cool. But what about the bridge-and-tunnel crowd? They don't want to schlep into Manhattan to see a musical about rats. They think Manhattan has too many rats already."

"Come on, Jerry," Susanna said impatiently. "It's not a musical about rats. It's a quote from Sherlock Holmes himself, about a mystery that would never be written about."

113

"*I* know that," Jerry retorted. "But *they* don't. And they're the ones who buy tickets to successful Broadway musicals. If they don't buy, it's not successful."

"Jerry's right," one of the members of the Giant Rat's gang said. "I've got a friend who works in the business office. Advance sales to the suburban theater clubs are a lot lower than expected. Management isn't doing anything about it, either. We may not even make Broadway. If by some miracle we do, don't count on a long run. And don't lose the name of your employment consultant."

Susanna sprang up, with fire in her eyes. "I do not believe you people!" she exclaimed. "This is a *great* play, with a fantastic score, and we're going to make it a hit. So what if we've had a few bad breaks? Are we going to let that stop us? No! Years from now, you're going to be bragging to people that you were in the original cast of *The Giant Rat of Sumatra.*"

"Yay, Susanna," Hector said. "That's the spirit we need."

Joe couldn't tell if he was being serious or sarcastic.

Al, the stagehand, appeared in the doorway and said, "We're getting ready to run through the transformation scene. Places, please."

114

Hector stood up and stretched. "Okay, boys and girls, time to earn our pay," he said.

Standing in the wings, Joe began to feel excited. He had watched this scene half a dozen times, but he was still captivated by the magic that transformed a London street into the shadowy interior of a sinister warehouse.

As the lighting changed in color and intensity, the turntable started to revolve. The set that represented the warehouse came into view. As it did, Joe saw a limp figure lying half on, half off the turntable, legs dragging along the floorboards. His first thought was that the trickster must be getting more use from the dummy.

Then Joe's eyes widened. As the figure drew closer, it began to look terribly familiar. Even in the dim light, Joe could not mistake the face of his brother.

With mounting horror, he saw that Frank was being dragged toward a wooden column, one of the platform supports. In another moment, his legs would be caught between the wall of the revolving set and the column.

He'd be crushed!

12 Sherlock Gets His Man

"Stop the turntable! *Now!*" Joe shouted.

Confused shouts drowned out Joe's. Clenching his jaw, he dashed out onto the stage. His left foot landed on the moving turntable. He lost his balance and almost fell. Flailing his arms, he recovered and sprinted to Frank's side. He grabbed him under the arms and tried to drag him back, out of danger. But Frank's limp body refused to budge.

Growing frantic, Joe glanced toward the column. It was less than a yard from Frank's legs now. What was keeping Frank from moving? Whatever it was, it *had* to give way! Joe grabbed a lungful of air, planted his feet, and pulled at Frank with every ounce of energy he had.

There was a loud ripping sound, and Joe fell backward. He sprang to his knees, still holding Frank's arms and ready to renew his effort. But Frank's legs were now on the turntable, out of harm's way. Well, mostly. There was a long rip down the left leg of his jeans and an ugly scratch on his calf from which drops of blood were starting to ooze.

The turntable shuddered to a halt. Joe shuddered, too, as he realized how narrowly his brother had escaped being maimed for life.

"Frank?" Joe said, bending down. "Frank, are you okay?"

Frank's eyes fluttered. He slowly raised one hand and touched the side of his head. "It hurts," he said in a weak voice.

"Don't move," Joe said urgently. "We'll get a doctor."

Frank shook his head, then winced with pain. "I'll be all right," he said. He shrugged away Joe's hand and lifted himself to a sitting position. Wincing, he examined the cut on his leg.

Bettina rushed over and cried out, "What happened? What's going on? Is he okay?"

"I must have fallen and hit my head," Frank told her. He grabbed Joe's shoulder and staggered to his feet. "I'm okay now. My brother tugged too hard and tore my jeans."

"If you're sure . . ." Bettina said, giving him a

doubtful look. She turned and called out, "Okay, everybody. Emergency's over. On with the rehearsal."

"I have to go," Joe said softly. "Are you sure you're okay?"

Frank gave him a tired nod. "It's just a scratch. I'll wash it and put some medication on it. We need to talk, though, first chance you get," he said.

"You bet," Joe replied.

O'Lunny rushed up. "Frank, Joe, what happened?"

"Frank will fill you in," Joe said. "Take care of him, will you?"

Frank put one hand on O'Lunny's shoulder, and the two walked slowly offstage.

It felt like forever, but finally Joe's scene with the Irregulars was finished. He rushed offstage, finding O'Lunny in the wings, talking with Hornby. When O'Lunny saw Joe, he said, "Frank's fine. I left him in the greenroom."

Joe expected to find Frank stretched out on the couch, resting. Instead, he was pacing up and down the room like a tiger at the zoo. His face brightened when Joe walked in.

"Let's get to work," he said.

"Sure, but first tell me what happened to you,"

Joe replied. "Did you really fall and hit your head?"

Frank shook his head, then winced. "No. Somebody did it for me. Here's what happened. I tried to track down who bought the ammonia, but no luck. So I came back to the theater to look up everybody's bios and check for some link among them. I went to the office, sat down at the computer, and started to boot up. And the next thing I know, I'm lying on the stage with a humongous headache."

"Somebody slugged you, then dragged you to the stage?" Joe asked.

"Right," Frank said. "But why? Because they don't like my aftershave? My hunch is that there's something on the computer I wasn't supposed to see. No, change that—there *was* something on the computer. Whoever slugged me is bound to have deleted whatever it was. Come on."

"Come on where?" Joe asked.

"To the office," Frank replied. "I want to see what it is that's important enough to get me knocked out."

Joe waited until they were inside the office, with the door closed, to ask, "Didn't you say the bad guy must have erased it?"

Frank smiled. "Like most people, you think that when you delete a file from a computer disk, you erase it. Wrong. All you erase is the directory listing that tells the computer where the file is. The *contents* of the file are still there, at least until the disk is reformatted or some other file gets saved in the same location."

Frank turned on the computer, typed in SHER-LOCK, and looked through the main directory. "Good," he said. "The diagnostic program they've got installed is one I've used before. Now, let's see. . . ."

As he entered a series of commands, he explained, "I'm trying to find out if any files or directories were deleted this afternoon. And the answer is . . . yes! KEYPERS.INS. Joe, do you see a blank disk anywhere? I'm going to copy this material so we can take a shot at deciphering it later at home."

Joe found a box of formatted disks and passed one to Frank. "Why not just read it now?" he asked.

"Because when you save a file, the computer sticks bits of it in any nooks and crannies that happen to be free," Frank replied. "Then, when you call up the file, the machine uses the directory listing to put it together again for you. But we don't *have* the detailed directory listing. All we know is which sectors the file's in. So we'll have to print them out, then hunt through a lot of garbage to find the strings we're after."

120

The disk drive whirred. Frank glanced up at Joe's face and laughed. "I didn't say it was going to be easy." He ejected the disk and put it in his pocket. "Let's get out of here before someone decides to hit both of us over the head!"

They left the theater. "I remember a good coffee shop down the street," Frank said. "Let's get something to eat."

"There it is," Joe said. "We used to eat here when Mom took us shopping. And it's still called Carol's." They went inside and slid into a booth. "We always had BLTs, remember?"

Frank nodded. As soon as the waitress appeared, he and Joe ordered BLTs and colas. She wrote down the order on her pad and left.

"I'm going to check our machine," Frank said. "Maybe Mr. Hiroto called."

He came back just as the sandwiches and drinks arrived. Once the waitress was gone, he said, "The flecks in Bag A were spray enamel."

"We knew that," Joe pointed out. "What about Bag B? The stuff from O'Lunny's sleeve?"

Frank let out an exasperated sigh. "Talcum powder, maybe in aerosol form," he reported. "Certainly not enamel. O'Lunny's in the clear."

Joe surprised himself by saying, "I'm glad to hear it. I like him. And I didn't want to think he was deliberately playing us for a couple of chumps."

"Me, neither," Frank replied. "So who does that leave? Li Wei had that meeting with Lestell in his limo. Hector has a great job waiting if *The Giant Rat* closes. And Gordean wants his pal, Will Robertson, to get Battenberg's part. Have I left anyone out?"

Joe shook his head and picked up the second half of his sandwich. "Not that I can think of. Let's finish up and get back. I want to go over my entrance cues again before tonight." He polished off the sandwich in three bites and drank down the last of the cola.

"You're becoming more of an actor than a detective," Frank said. "Watch it—I might have to go onstage, too, so we stay a team. And I bet if I did, I'd blow your doors off."

Deadpan, Joe said, "Sorry. Blowing doors off is part of the Big Bad Wolf's business. And his role has already been cast. Toss you for the check?"

"The prices haven't changed either," Frank said. "This is my treat."

Back at the theater, Joe grabbed his script and went in search of Hector. He found him in the greenroom with the rest of the Irregulars.

"My man," Hector said expansively. "Come on in. I was just giving a sermon about good luck."

"Oh? Why?" Joe asked.

Hector smiled. "Here's the skinny. The same

day I accepted this role, I was offered a big part in a new TV series. Was I steamed! But I'd already made a commitment, so there I was."

"Come on, Hector, what's the punchline?" Max grumbled.

"This. I just spoke to my agent." Hector paused, letting the tension build. "And the network's canned the series. Totally down the tubes. They said they didn't want any more crime shows. If I'd ditched this part to take that one—and you can bet I was tempted—I'd be back programming computers now. Instead, I've got a terrific role in a terrific musical. So you see? Sometimes, keeping your word is not only good for your soul, but good for your career."

"You know what's weird, though?" Susanna said. "According to a friend of mine on the Coast, a few days ago one of the studios offered Battenberg a major supporting role in a flick that's going into production three weeks from now, and he still hasn't said yes or no."

"He's probably waiting to see how the tryouts go," Max said. "If *Rat* looks like a hit, he'll stay, and if not, he'll split."

"And break his contract?" Susanna asked. "I don't think so. He'd never work on Broadway again. No, I think Battenberg will decline. But he just can't stand turning down a juicy movie role."

Joe thought fast. If Hector had told the truth

about the cancellation of the TV series—and why wouldn't he?—then his motive for being the trickster had just evaporated. And if Susanna's gossip was accurate, a new suspect had just surfaced: Battenberg himself, the victim of most of the dirty tricks. He definitely had a strong motive to see *The Giant Rat* fail, and fail quickly.

Frank was taking another look at the light board. The masking tape labels were illegible. How did anyone know which switch controlled what? He was scratching his head when O'Lunny came over to him.

"I've been thinking about what happened this afternoon," O'Lunny said. "How are you feeling?"

"I'm fine," Frank said. "I've got a hard head."

O'Lunny hesitated. "Frank . . . when I asked you and Joe for help, I never imagined that I'd be putting you in such danger. I don't think I can accept that responsibility. If anything happened to you or Joe, how could I face your father and mother? I'm going to have to ask you to give up your investigation."

Frank looked at him in surprise. O'Lunny's face had new strain lines on it, and his cheeks sagged. He looked like someone who badly needed a few days' rest.

"You're both doing a wonderful job," O'Lunny

continued. "It's not that. But how could I face your father? I'm afraid you'll have to drop it."

"I'm sorry to hear this," Frank said, trying to hide his surprise. "But I see your point. Could you do Joe a favor, though? It'd break his heart not to be in the play tonight, and I'd really like to watch from backstage."

"No, no, that's fine," O'Lunny said. "And thanks for being so understanding. Well, that's one less worry. If only I could deal with the others as easily. We'll talk later."

Watching him walk away, Frank wondered, *Why* did O'Lunny want them off the case? To keep them safe, as he had said? Or to keep them from getting any closer to the truth?

Suddenly Frank felt someone grab him by the collar. He spun around. It was Battenberg, wearing the caped overcoat and deerstalker cap of Sherlock Holmes.

"What do you—" Frank started to demand.

In a voice that rang through the theater, Battenberg called, "Over here, Officer. Quickly! Here's your villain!"

13 A Shot in the Dark

Battenberg tightened his hold on Frank's shirt collar while a police officer came hurrying toward them. The policeman had his hand on the butt of his service revolver and wore a determined expression.

"We got a call to 911," the officer said. "A report of a dangerous intruder."

"It was I who called," Battenberg announced to the gathering crowd. "Once I deduced the identity of the miscreant, I judged it time to hand responsibility over to Scotland Yard. Or, in this case, the Bayport Police Department."

Someone in the crowd muttered, "Wacko."

"You can let him go, sir," the police officer said to Battenberg. "I'll handle this."

To Frank, he said, "Can I see some ID, sir? Are you aware that this part of the theater is off-limits to the public?"

Frank reached slowly for his wallet and produced his driver's license. As the officer took down the information from it, Frank said, "Chief Collig will vouch for me, Officer. And I'm not an intruder. Donald O'Lunny, the author and co-producer of the play, asked me to serve as his assistant."

Battenberg turned away from Frank to face the crowd. "It was quite elementary," he announced. "I simply applied the principle of the Dog in the Night, from Arthur Conan Doyle's story 'The Hound of the Baskervilles.' In that case, what aroused Holmes's suspicions was that the dog did nothing in the night."

Hector asked, "Are you saying you suspect Frank because he hasn't done anything?"

Battenberg gave him a superior smile. "Exactly, my dear chap. Some villain has been trying to destroy our play, correct? And he certainly isn't going to announce his identity by behaving in a suspicious manner, correct? So I simply looked around for the person whose manner was least suspicious. And here he is."

Susanna looked over at Frank and rolled her eyes. Then she twirled her forefinger near her temple. Frank grinned back.

Hornby came rushing up. "Now what?" he demanded.

Three or four people at once tried to explain. Hornby swallowed an antacid tablet, then said, "Officer? What's the problem here?"

"Seems to be a misunderstanding," the police officer said. He indicated Battenberg. "This gentleman thought that Mr. Hardy was an unauthorized intruder. According to Mr. Hardy, he's working here."

"Of course he is," Hornby said. "I'm directing this show, and I take full responsibility, Officer. Here's my card."

Hornby turned to Battenberg and continued, "As for you, Charles, you're letting your role as Holmes go to your head. Would you please restrict your urge to play detective to the stage?"

Battenberg drew himself up and threw his head back, as if he were posing for his portrait. Stiffly, he said, "You seem to forget that I am the key person in this production, Gilbert. This is not merely my opinion, it is my official status in this company. And as the key person, I consider it my duty to do whatever I must to safeguard the welfare of the production. Whatever the personal cost, I shall not shirk that duty."

Battenberg turned and stalked away. There was a smattering of applause from the crowd.

The police officer looked over at Frank with a hint of a grin and said, "I guess actors have to be a little bigger than life, huh, Mr. Hardy?"

"It sure looks that way," Frank replied.

Hornby scowled at the circle of onlookers. "Are you forgetting that we have a show to put on?" he demanded.

The crowd began to drift away. Before walking off, Hornby turned to Frank and said, "Watch your step, young man. Charles was clearly out of line, but that doesn't mean I'm happy about your presence. We have no room backstage for sightseers."

"Yes, sir," Frank said. He moved off in the opposite direction, trying to keep out of Hornby's way. Though O'Lunny had removed him from the case, Frank had no intention of actually dropping the investigation. He kept his eye out for anything that seemed out of the ordinary. But what did "out of the ordinary" mean, in a setting like this? There were people wandering around dressed as nineteenth-century gangsters, with clubs and even pistols in their belts. Was that ordinary? And what about someone who looked and dressed exactly like Sherlock Holmes and seemed half convinced that he was Sherlock Holmes? Was that ordinary?

As he crossed the back of the stage, Frank

saw O'Lunny in conversation with Li Wei. They both looked glum. Frank went over and joined them.

O'Lunny glanced at Frank and said, "It never rains, but it pours. Li Wei, tell Frank what you just told me."

"*Rat* is in very big trouble," Li Wei said. "I met this morning with someone who is very well placed to know what is happening. Gilbert Hornby's organization has been doing a terrible job of promoting the play. There are practically no advance sales. Unless something is done, and done quickly, we'll never even reach Broadway."

"But what can we do?" O'Lunny demanded. "It seems hopeless."

"Some of the backers are talking seriously about getting a new producer," Li Wei said. "I don't need to mention names. But if it's going to do any good, it must happen before *Rat* gets a reputation as a failure. All these accidents and incidents are destroying any chance we have of saving the play. Donald, can't you do anything to stop them?"

O'Lunny met Frank's eye as he said, "I'll do everything I can."

"Please," Li Wei said. She started to walk away, then turned to add, "It's very important, to all of us."

After a moment O'Lunny said, "Frank, I take back what I said before. Will you and Joe carry on with your investigation? You can see how urgent it is. Just be extra careful that you don't get hurt. Please," O'Lunny finished, his voice wavering with emotion.

"You can count on us," Frank said. "Now, I'd better go find Joe and fill him in."

Joe was in the men's dressing room, struggling with his makeup. Frank called from the doorway, and Joe joined him in the hall. In a low voice Frank told him the latest developments. "You see what this all means?" he concluded. "Li Wei *does* have a link to Lestell, but that doesn't give her a motive to sabotage the play. She sincerely wants it to be a success. So she's off our suspect list, too."

Joe rubbed his chin, then looked with dismay at the tan makeup on his hand. "So who's left?" he asked. "Battenberg, that's who," he said, answering his own question. Joe quickly told Frank his latest thoughts about Battenberg as a suspect. "Still, I don't accept the motive. Why would he want to get out of the play, just to be in some movie? He lives and breathes Sherlock Holmes. I bet he even wears that funny Holmes cap in the shower."

"Which brings us down to zero suspects,"

Frank said. "Our only hope is to catch the trickster redhanded. But face it, we can't be everywhere at once."

"Then what do we do?" Joe demanded. Frank didn't answer. Joe noticed his brother seemed to be miles away, so he nudged him and asked again.

Frank's face broke into a grin. "We do what Sherlock Holmes would do. We call in the Baker Street Irregulars!"

"Why didn't I think of that?" Joe mumbled as they went off in search of Hector. He was in the greenroom with Susanna. Frank started to explain what they wanted.

After the first couple of sentences, Susanna interrupted. "You're detectives? I knew it had to be something like that."

"I figured something was up," Hector said. "Don't take this the wrong way, but, Frank, you're not the go-fer type, and sorry, Joe, but you're no actor."

Joe's face fell, but this was no time for hurt feelings.

"Will you help? You and the others?" Frank asked.

"You can count on us," Hector replied. "Anything unusual, we'll let you know right away."

"And good hunting!" Susanna said.

* * *

On the stage, Holmes stood in his sitting room, playing a haunting melody on his violin.

Frank was in the wings, between Susanna and Joe. "You know, Battenberg's really good," he whispered to Susanna. "Where did he learn to play the violin?"

"It's a recording," she replied. "It's being broadcast to a radio receiver under his chair. You're right, though, in a way. He fakes pretty well."

The music was interrupted by the arrival of a client. The visitor explained that he was a shipowner being blackmailed by the Sumatra Rats. He was scheduled to deliver a payoff that afternoon, in the East End. Would Holmes watch secretly and catch the villains in the act of collecting the money?

What the audience knew, and Holmes supposedly didn't, was that the shipowner was really the Giant Rat himself, in disguise. He had devised a fiendish plot to kidnap Holmes and Watson, or if necessary, to kill them.

Once more the scene changed to the dank shadowy docklands warehouse that was the headquarters of the Sumatra Rats. After a song in which the Giant Rat made hair-raising threats about what he was planning to do to Holmes, some of the gang hid in ambush near the entrance. But at that moment Holmes and Watson, revolvers in hand, suddenly appeared from the other direction.

"Hands up, please," Holmes said. "A fine rat trap, wouldn't you say, Watson?"

From where he was standing, Holmes couldn't see the character played by Robertson. Robertson stealthily drew a club from his belt, then jumped out to aim a blow at Holmes's head.

Holmes reacted instantly. He aimed his revolver over his attacker's head and pulled the trigger. There was a loud *bang!*

Frank couldn't quite believe what he saw next.

A few inches above Robertson's head, a window shattered, and shards of glass rained down on the actor.

14 A Message from the Beyond

Susanna grabbed Frank's arm. "That wasn't a blank, that was a real bullet!"

Onstage all the actors were paralyzed with shock. Robertson was staring up at the shattered window. Battenberg was staring down at the revolver in his hand. Then they all seemed to remember they were in a play and that hundreds of spectators were watching every move they made.

"That was just a warning," Battenberg ad-libbed. "Behave yourself, or next time I may aim lower."

"Right you are, guv'ner," Robertson replied. He gingerly placed his club on the ground, then raised his hands.

"Quick—where are the guns and ammunition kept?" Frank asked Susanna in a whisper.

"Stage right, in a cabinet near Bettina's desk," Susanna replied. "But it's always locked. I don't see how—"

Frank didn't wait for the end of her sentence. "Come on, Joe," he said, walking quickly toward the rear of the stage. They passed behind the set, then made their way forward to the stage manager's station. Bettina was dividing her attention between the action on the stage and a lanky bearded man of about forty.

"I can't explain it," the man was saying. "We don't even have any live ammunition. Not a single round. Why would we?"

"Face it, Alex," Bettina said. "It wasn't a blank that blew that hole in the set. Either it was an oversight or someone played a very dangerous prank. I want you to check every cartridge in every gun we have . . . and do it before the next act. Okay?"

"You bet," Alex said. He went over to a steel cabinet fastened to the wall and unlocked the door.

Frank stepped up to the manager and said, "Bettina, Donald O'Lunny asked me to find out as much as I can about this accident. Are the revolvers always kept locked up?"

"They certainly are," Bettina replied. "When-

136

ever they're needed onstage, Alex, our props manager, personally hands each one to the actor who's supposed to carry it. And at the end of the scene, he collects them and puts them back in the cabinet."

"Does a particular actor always get the same gun?" Joe asked.

Bettina nodded. "That's right. They're different sizes and types. We don't want to confuse anybody."

"And who has a key to the cabinet?" Frank asked.

Bettina's face hardened. "I thought it would come to this," she said defensively. "I do. So does Alex. That's it. Make of it what you will."

"Aren't there any other copies?" Joe asked. "Maybe a spare somewhere?"

"Well, yes, we have a duplicate set of keys in the office, in case one gets lost," Bettina replied. "But they're always kept locked up."

Frank asked, "Do you have any idea how that live round got into Battenberg's revolver?"

"I wish I did," Bettina said. "I'll tell you one thing—it wasn't Battenberg who put it there. The guy is practically phobic about guns. I hear he goes and scrubs his hands after every scene where he has to even touch one. I can't imagine him unloading a blank and putting in a live cartridge."

137

She held up her hand, then listened intently to her headset. "Sorry, guys," she said hastily. "Duty calls." She turned back to face the stage.

Frank and Joe got into a huddle. "The key to the cabinet is in the office," Joe pointed out.

"The key to the whole case is in the office," Frank retorted. "That's where somebody hocussed the complimentary-ticket program, somebody typed and printed that note that was supposed to lure Battenberg into falling through the trapdoor . . ."

"And somebody knocked you out, then erased that computer file," Joe concluded. "Okay, next question—who, besides us, has a key to the office? Mila, obviously. O'Lunny, unless he gave you his only key."

"I know Hornby does," Frank said. "He came in while I was there this morning. He wasn't happy to find me there."

"I'd like to search the place more carefully," Joe said.

"No better time than now," Frank replied. "No one's likely to interrupt us while the play's going on."

Once again they circled behind the set. They were turning into the corridor that led to the office when O'Lunny intercepted them.

"We can't go on like this," he announced. "I'm going to insist we suspend the rest of the performances here in Bayport, and I'm seriously inclined to cancel the run on Broadway as well."

"Why?" Joe asked.

"How can you ask?" O'Lunny retorted. "You saw what just happened. It was only by pure chance that Will Robertson wasn't killed! Before this, I thought we were dealing with a mere prankster. Now I realize that our opponent is a cold, ruthless murderer."

"Will you wait a little longer before you do something as drastic as closing the show?" Frank asked. "I can't promise anything, but I think we're close to cracking the case."

O'Lunny stared at him. "You are? That's wonderful, if it's true. Can you tell me—"

"I'm afraid not," Frank said, shaking his head. "Not yet. One question, though. Who has keys to the production office?"

The playwright's eyes widened. "Why, I do, of course, and our secretary, Mila, and Gilbert Hornby."

"Anyone else?" Joe asked. "What about Bettina?"

"No, she doesn't need one," O'Lunny replied. "And I gave you fellows the spare. Why?"

"We'll explain later," Frank promised. "Right now, we have work to do."

"So do I," O'Lunny said. "I'll look for you later."

As the Hardys continued down the hall to the office, Joe said in a low voice, "It's got to be Hornby, Frank. Unless you think Mila is the guilty one. Personally, I don't see her knocking you out, then carrying or dragging you to the stage."

"I don't either," Frank admitted. "But she could be working with somebody. I know Hornby looks like a more likely candidate. But why would he try to wreck his own play, when he's got so much at stake?"

"I have no idea," Joe replied. "But remember what Holmes said."

Frank groaned. "Oh, please, not the Dog in the Night again!"

"Nope," Joe said. "I mean, 'Once you eliminate the possible, what remains, however improbable, is the truth.' That's not word for word, but it's close enough."

Frank gave his brother an admiring glance, then unlocked the office door. Once they were inside, he relocked it. If anyone came in on him this time, he wanted a few seconds warning.

"This shouldn't take long," he told Joe. "Why don't you take the file cabinet and I'll take the desk."

They both got to work. Frank barely had time to go through the center drawer of the desk when Joe cried, "Frank, look at this!"

Frank joined Joe at the file cabinet. At the very back of the bottom drawer, behind the hanging files, was a twisted-up shopping bag from Value Plus. Joe pulled it out and looked inside.

"A plastic raincoat, a can of white spray enamel," he announced, "and a cash register receipt that lists a bottle of ammonia and a spool of nylon leader."

Frank beamed. "That's great evidence, Joe. The only thing is, will the clerk at the discount store remember the purchases? All of the items are pretty ordinary, even if the combination is weird."

"Good point," Joe said. "But who's our mystery shopper? Hornby? We still don't have the ghost of a motive for him."

Frank looked around the office. On the desk next to the computer, the red light was blinking on the answering machine. Frank went over and pressed Play, then kept his finger ready on the Fast Forward button.

"Hello, I'm calling about complimentary seats . . ." *Click, whirr.*

"This is Mike Seward, at the *Journal.* I'd like to set up some interviews . . ." *Click, whirr.*

"Mila, it's Inessa. Give me a call . . ." *Click, whirr.*

Joe said, "Come on. This is a waste of time."
Frank held his finger up to his lips.

141

"Mr. Hornby, this is Alice, at the Beyond the Horizon Agency. I have a confirmation on your rental of the Marston villa on Aruba for next week. As I told you, the price includes the use of a car and the services of a maid and cook. I hope you enjoy your stay. Please call me if you have any questions. And have a lovely trip. Goodbye." Alice hung up, and the machine fell silent.

Joe stared at Frank. "Aruba? Next week? But Frank, *Rat* still might make it to Broadway. What producer-director would want to miss that?"

"One who already knows that it's not going to happen," Frank said. "One who's going to make sure that it doesn't happen."

"But why?" Joe demanded.

"Joe, that computer file," Frank said. "The one labeled KEYPERS.INS. That stands for 'Key Person Insurance.' It's the policy that people have been talking about. It's what Battenberg meant when he said he was the key person in the production. If Battenberg can't perform—if he breaks a leg falling through a trapdoor or has a sandbag fall on his head—Hornby collects a million dollars! Hornby must have been the one who deleted that file that we retrieved. He didn't want anyone to know he'd make out like a bandit if something happened to Battenberg. How's that for a motive?"

"It'll do," Joe said. "But, Frank—we've got to

stop him! He must be getting desperate. Who knows what he'll do to Battenberg next?''

A key turned in the lock. Frank and Joe looked around as the door opened. Hornby was standing with his hand on the knob and a look of surprise on his face. His thick black eyebrows lowered into a suspicious scowl as he took in Frank's expression. Then he looked over at Joe and saw the plastic bag in his hands.

Before Frank and Joe could react, Hornby jumped back, slammed the door shut, and twisted the key in the lock. Frank and Joe were locked in. And Hornby was getting away.

15 The Game's Afoot

Frank ran to the door and jammed the key into the old-fashioned lock. It refused to go more than halfway in. Frank jiggled it, then tried twisting the knob. No good. Hornby must have left *his* key in the lock on the outside of the door. It was blocking Frank's key from going in.

"Hurry!" Joe said.

Frank held up a hand for silence. He fished out his pocketknife from his hip pocket and opened a pointed blade meant for removing pebbles from a horse's hoof. Getting down on one knee, he peered into the keyhole.

The light from the corridor outlined the shape of the other key. Delicately, Frank inserted the blade and wedged the point next to the flat extension of the key. Taking a deep breath, he twisted the blade a fraction of an inch. The key clattered to the floor outside.

"Piece of cake," Frank said. He sprang to his feet and used his own key to unlock the door. "Now let's get that guy!"

They dashed out into the hallway. "He'll be gone by now," Joe said.

Frank shook his head. "He thinks we're still locked up. He won't want to call attention to himself. I'm betting he's somewhere backstage."

Hector intercepted them. "Hey, what's going on?" he asked. "I just ran into Hornby, and, man, is he acting weird."

"He's the one who's been pulling the dirty tricks," Joe said quickly. "Where is he?"

"I saw him a minute ago behind the set," Hector said. "You want me to help?"

"No," Frank said, clapping him on the shoulder. "Stay here and watch for him, in case he gives us the slip."

Frank and Joe ran toward the rear of the stage. The warehouse set loomed above them, looking even spookier than usual in the faint glow of the work lights.

Joe touched Frank on the shoulder and pointed. About fifteen feet away, Hornby was kneeling next to a flight of iron stairs that led to the upper level of the set. It looked as if he was tying something to the rod that supported the handrail.

The Hardys started to creep up on Hornby, but he must have sensed something. He took one quick look over his shoulder, then jumped to his feet and started running up the stairs.

Frank and Joe sprinted after him. Frank reached the stairs first. On the third step, something snagged his foot. He went flying forward. His knee banged into the edge of a stair. He threw his hands out just in time to keep his chin from smashing against another step.

"Joe, watch out," Frank called over his shoulder, as he pulled himself to his feet and started running up the stairs again. "It's booby-trapped."

At the top of the stairs, Frank found himself at one end of a long narrow metal catwalk. Burlap-covered bales of merchandise were stacked high against the wall.

Hornby was already near the far end of the catwalk. He looked back and saw Frank. His face twisted, and he reached over and grabbed a bale as big as a washing machine. He raised it high over his head. Then he heaved it down the catwalk at Frank.

Frank dropped into a crouch. The bale sailed over his head. Too late, he remembered that Joe was right behind him. He turned, expecting to see Joe crushed under the weight of the bale.

He was standing with the bale clasped in his arms. "Stage prop," he said, with a quick grin. "It can't weigh more than a pound or two."

Joe tossed the bale behind him and edged past Frank, then broke into a run, with Frank close behind. At the far end of the catwalk was another set of iron stairs. Hornby clattered down them three at a time, then ran toward the edge of the set.

Joe and Frank raced after him. A moment later they were in the sitting room of Holmes's flat at 221B Baker Street. From the other side of the painted canvas walls, Joe heard a chorus of police constables singing, "If you want to meet the reason that crime doesn't pay . . ."

Dodging the overstuffed furniture, Hornby ran across the room. Joe was only a few feet behind him and gaining. Desperate, Hornby dashed over to a door in the set wall, flung it open, and rushed through. Joe darted after him . . . and landed in the middle of a startled group of singing bobbies. A gasp went up from the audience.

True pros, the singing police didn't miss a note. They shifted their positions to screen Joe and Hornby from the auditorium. Joe did his best to block out the rows and rows of staring eyes in the audience. Grabbing Hornby, he got him in a hammerlock and hustled him offstage.

"Joe, what—" O'Lunny exclaimed.

"Here's your trickster," Joe panted.

O'Lunny's jaw dropped. "Gilbert? But why?" he demanded, as Frank hurried to join them.

"He was planning to put Battenberg out of commission, then collect the million dollars in insurance," Frank said. "We'll tell you all about it later."

After the final curtain, the cast crowded into the greenroom. Rumors had been flying around backstage since Joe's spectacular capture of Hornby.

O'Lunny climbed up onto a chair and said, "We've all been upset by the malicious incidents that have been happening the last few days. They had to stop, before they destroyed our play. So I asked Frank and Joe Hardy to go undercover and find the person responsible. And that's just what they did. Frank, Joe?"

The Hardys took turns explaining what Hornby had done and why.

"The poor advance sales convinced him that *Rat* was going to be a flop," Joe said. "That made the insurance money very tempting."

"The rat," Hector said. "Oops, sorry—I mean, the skunk! But if his real target was Charles, why did he mess up the complimentary tickets and put ammonia in the fog machine and all?"

"Smoke screen," Frank replied. "If the insurance company investigated, he must have hoped that they'd see Battenberg's injury as part of a general run of bad luck and incompetence."

Susanna asked, "What happens now?"

O'Lunny cleared his throat. "That's up to our lawyer and the local police," he said. "Needless to say, Gilbert Hornby is no longer connected to this production in any way."

"What I really meant," Susanna said, "was, what happens to the show?"

"Perhaps I can help answer that," came a voice from the doorway.

Frank looked around. Tertius Lestell was standing there, wearing a white suit, a raccoon coat, and a bowler hat. Li Wei was next to him.

"I have heard about your troubles," Lestell said. "I'd like to offer you whatever help I and my organization can give. Believe me, it's not charity on my part. I'm convinced that, properly handled, you have a hit on your hands, and I want to be associated with it."

He looked over at Frank and Joe. "For a start, think of the headlines," he said with a sly smile. "'Teen Sleuths Capture Crook Onstage During Sherlock Musical.' That alone will boost ticket sales fifteen percent."

Battenberg was over near the wall. He stepped forward and said, "Tertius, I'm delighted that you're joining us. I should tell you that I've had grave suspicions of Gilbert Hornby for some time now."

"Really?" Gordean drawled. "Then why did you make that ridiculous and very public accusation against Frank Hardy?"

Battenberg gave him a superior smile. "A ruse, my dear fellow," he said. "By seeming to suspect my young colleague here, I hoped to lull Gilbert into making a careless mistake. And it worked."

Straining to keep a straight face, Frank looked over at Hector and Susanna. They were both working hard not to break down into laughter.

Mila rushed in. "Hey, everybody," she said loudly. "I just caught the eleven o'clock news on Channel Six. Their theater critic was at tonight's performance, and he loved it. He said the show's guaranteed to be a hit!"

The room broke out in cheers. Joe let out an ear-piercing whistle. When the noise died down, Lestell said, "Congratulations. In celebration, I'd like you all to be my guests for a late supper at a restaurant near here, Au Vieux Port. There'll be cars outside the theater in fifteen minutes."

"So all those incidents were Hornby's work?" asked Susanna, who was sitting next to Frank at a long table covered in white linen.

Frank looked up from his crabmeat and calamari cocktail. Before answering, he glanced